Also by M.L. Bullock

Desert Queen Saga
The Tale of Nefret
The Falcon Rises
The Kingdom of Nefertiti
The Song of the Bee Eater

Gulf Coast Paranormal Trilogy Series
Ghosted
Haunted
Dead
Spooked
Paranormal

Haunting Passions
Her Haunted Heart

Scary Fall Stories
Horrible Little Things

Seven Sisters
Seven Sisters
Ghost on a Swing

Twelve to Midnight
Mary Twelves
Pieces of Twelves

Standalone
Christmas at Seven Sisters
Delivered Me From Evil

Watch for more at www.mlbullock.com.

THE KINGDOM OF NEFERTITI

By M.L. Bullock

1

To Nicole, my cousin and fan of my first story, "Eyes in the Fire." We
scared ourselves silly!
All my love, Mimi

Table of Contents

I hear thy voice, O turtle dove

The dawn is all aglow.

Weary am I with love, with love, Oh, whither shall I go?

Not so, O beauteous bird above

Is joy to be denied

For I have found my dear, my love; And I am by his side.

We wander forth, and hand in hand

Through flowery ways we go

I am the fairest in the land, for he has called me so.

—Anonymous Poet, 1580-1085 BC

Chapter One

*S*acred Markings—Astora

My Meshwesh husband's tribesman raised his bushy eyebrows at me when he saw my new sacred markings. The scrolling stars were now emblazoned across my forehead, and I refused to wear a headcloth to hide them while they healed. I was not ashamed! Let the people know that I had power! In fact, let them fear me. Orba left my presence as quickly as he came, forgetting what he wanted to say to me. I laughed at his back. Weak man.

Good, I thought, *I was in no mood for his petty complaints today.*

I had bigger things to think about. I let my mind wander as I sewed the last stitches on the robe's hem. How fortunate that I had saved this fine fabric. It would prove useful since no one had seen it except my husband, Omel, who had given it to me. I could trust him. I rubbed the soft silk and touched it absently to my cheek.

I missed Omel. It had been a long time since we had lain together, shared bread, or even spoken to one another. Our relationship was not a romance like the one I had dreamed of as a young girl, but it was practical and comfortable. When I married him, I had been sure we were destined for greatness. This painful separation was all thanks to the half-breed girl who called herself both mekhma and Queen of Egypt. I snorted at the idea. The world had far too many queens these days. How could it be that she, a commoner from an obscure bloodline, could be queen? I hissed at the thought of my husband's niece wielding power—power she would undoubtedly use against us. How could she deny him rulership of the Meshwesh? Pah was of no use to anyone, and with Alexio's interference I could neither visit her nor speak with her.

Omel and I had given so much for these people to have received so little in recognition and honor. Did my husband not deserve honor? It was his tribe that saved the Meshwesh. They were the bravest and fastest warriors in the Red Lands, and yet the one-armed king still reigned, thanks to his daughter's influence, no doubt.

And I? I had lost Suri—my only son—my heart and breath. My reason for living. Everything I had done until that day had been for him. He had only begun to ride with his father, to learn how to rule. Now he was no more.

When I agreed to marry Omel, long before Suri entered this world, I had prepared the way for my dear son. Omel had promised to put all his sons aside for mine, for I had been sure I would have a son. He had easily agreed, for he had not loved his other sons' mothers as he loved me. He had been handfasted twice before me. One woman had died in childbirth, another of a mysterious fever.

How easy that had been!

No one brought me Suri's body to bury or even presented me with a clipping of his hair. I begged Omel to retrieve him, but he refused, saying it would do no good. I assumed that there was not much left of my son's young body. My husband's refusal made me hate the Meshwesh even more.

To this day, no one recognized Suri's sacrifice. He was a king's son, after all. No one missed him. None of his brothers or cousins mentioned his name. It was no secret that they had not loved my child. Even my husband did not mention his name, except on the occasion that I presented him with a votive dedicated to Suri. I could then see the emotion in his eyes and feel his brokenness. We held one another for a long while, but then he was gone again. Now I had empty arms, and the pain of the loss was so deep that it had stolen even my tears. I would no longer touch my son's warm brown skin or shove his dark, silky hair out of his eyes as he swatted my hands away. I would no longer need to make honey cakes every day for his hungry stomach or wash his feet at night.

I accidentally stabbed myself with the needle and quickly shoved the finger in my mouth to stop the bleeding. I could not stain this garment. The spilled blood could reverse the magic or present a result I did not expect. What I was doing was dangerous enough. I snatched up the robe and walked inside my home. The light had faded, and I had much to do. It was usually about this time of day when my son would burst into our tent and ply me with kisses for food.

No, I would never forget Suri. In fact, I would avenge him if it was with the last breath I took.

I had taken my blood vengeance on the Kiffians for their part in his death. I had simply stolen a cloak from one of their dead and snuck into their city once the gate had been breached. Very few women and children were in their camp, and I suspected many were merely prisoners, but I found a boy-child who had the look of one of the Kiffian giants. I found him and quickly killed him. When his screaming mother charged at me, I killed her too. By then, the chaos of the battle had crept into their small encampment in the west of Zerzura, and no one thought anything else about me. In fact, no one even knew I had left the wagons. Except perhaps Orba, who had dogged my every step. Or so he thought. I smiled as I smoothed the robe.

What pretty fabric! Rose gold silk with a shimmer of metallic thread. The perfect outfit for a seductive dancer. It had been a thoughtful gift, but it hardly made up for the loss of my son. My husband had showered me with Kiffian plunder before he left for Thebes.

Poor Omel. I had no illusions when it came to him. He married me because the blood of Neferue, the daughter of Hatshepsut, the long-dead Queen of Egypt, flowed through my veins. She had been a true queen! My Egyptian family had long since fallen out of power, but unlike them, I would not deny the blood that coursed through my veins. And I planned to be a queen of another sort.

I had not told Omel of my plans beyond a few whispers on our pillow. As always, he warned me about my scheming, but I knew he appreciated my work. Besides, he would know soon enough, for he would see me. The less he knew at this crucial juncture, the better.

He had seen my painted skin bring the power he desired time and time again, yet this power frightened him. Men had frail souls. What a joke of the gods! They gave men the physical strength and women the mind of leopards, intelligent, fast, and able to make a decision—even a deadly one when needed.

If only I'd had the power to kill Orba! That would have solved many problems. But his magic always overwhelmed me. Sometimes it blinded my second sight, and other times it came at me in waves and made me physically sick. Once I thought he had poisoned me, so sick was I, but it was only magic. Gnarly, old Meshwesh magic. But it was no true match for one who had the power of Egypt coursing through her body!

I needed to leave, at least for a little while. If Omel could not come to me, I would go to him. He needed me—of that I was sure. And my Suri needed his blood vengeance, or he would dwell in darkness for all eternity. The debt must be paid, and it must be paid with the blood of Semkah's children! Pah had the mind of an idiot now. Killing her would be doing her a favor. She had been useful in the past, but not anymore. It was Nefret, the upstart, who must pay the price for Suri. Her father's stubbornness had caused this! How long had Omel warned him to accept Egypt's hand of protection? If it had not been for Semkah, we would not have been in Timia when the Kiffians stormed across that oasis. If it had not been for Semkah, Suri would be alive—my son would have breath in his body. Now he was no more.

And that was why I called the little boy to me from my window.

I spotted him after I finished folding the robe. I smiled at him in an attempt to allay his fears. My tattoos frightened children, but I had a friendly smile and wide, dark eyes—eyes that children seemed to trust if I wanted them to. Ah...I knew what to do. I picked up Suri's old toy and walked to the doorway. I tapped on the toy goatskin drum and offered the cautious boy a chance to play with it. As I did, I surreptitiously glanced around me to make sure no one saw me. It was dusk now, and the approaching darkness cast purple shadows on the white stone buildings and walls of Zerzura. A lute played tumbling notes a few doors down. I could smell chula bread cooking somewhere. The boy stepped closer—he was only a few feet away now.

"Sumer! Come to me, son!" the boy's stupid mother called to him from a nearby doorway. The boy smiled at me once and then turned and ran home through the white stone arch.

"Curse you, child," I muttered under my breath, scowling at his shadow. I stormed inside my home and flopped in a chair until opportunity brought me another warm body. Another child, a girl-child, came into my home unbidden and unwelcome. Intrigued by her boldness, I did not beat her or turn her out.

"Astora? I am Ziza. My mother has sent me to find you. She says my sister Amon is not well. Will you come see her?"

Cautiously I asked, "Why doesn't she call Leela? I am no camp healer. Leela will be happy to heal your wretched sister." I felt sullen and petulant, not realizing the gift the goddess had sent me.

"She does not trust Leela, Astora. She says she trusts only you."

Curious now, I asked, "Does she indeed? Who is your mother?"

"Mareta. You know her. She brings you doves sometimes and the purple flowers that make ink. She says you know how to make the water flow, but I am not sure what she means."

Finally, I recognized the hand of the goddess at work! The girl's mention of the flow of water was a secret phrase that only another acolyte of Ahurani would know. I had thought to take the boy's blood, but it was the girl's blood that the goddess wanted—and she had sent another servant to convey that message to me. "Go now, Ziza. Tell your mother to come to me at once. There can be no delay. If she wants her child healed, she must pay the price. And you must return with her." Thoughtfully I added, "Tell your mother that the flowing water needs a rock to wash over." A true follower would understand my meaning.

Confused but not stupid enough to ask more questions, the girl sprinted from the tent to tell her mother the good news. While I waited, for I was convinced she would return, I prepared the things I would need. A small, gold-handled knife, two leather straps with the sacred knots tied into it, and a small offering bowl with a lid. The bowl was made of green jade, something not often seen in the Red Lands or even in the White City of Zerzura for all its hidden treasures. No, this gift came from my father's homeland, and its beauty and craftsmanship rivaled any Egyptian example. It was Persian-made, by the hand of someone who understood and respected the dying magic. I had dwelt there for a time as a girl. It was a good place to live—until I was cast out. One day, I would return in victory, taking my Meshwesh husband with me. Then he would see true power!

"Step inside, please," I called to the woman without looking up from my table. She lingered outside my door, and I heard her gasp in surprise. I did not bother to explain to her that I had heard her sandals on the stones outside and needed no magic to perceive her approach. I could tell she was easily impressed. That both pleased and saddened me.

I welcomed her inside and pointed to the table. I recognized Mareta but had not spoken to her much before this day. She had a square face, small, pale brown eyes, and a sleeping, plainly sick child in her arms.

I wondered how she would react when I demanded the due price for my healing magic. Fortunately for her, I did not need to kill the girl—not today. All I needed was her blood—at least a small bowl full.

Rather than alarm the sick child or her sister, I spoke to Mareta in the old language. "I need your daughter's blood. The goddess requires it."

"Which daughter? This one is sick."

"I need good blood, so this one. Ziza is her name?" The girl looked from her mother to me, as hearing her name mentioned must have surprised her. With a nod, Mareta laid the sick child on the table. Without hesitation, she clapped her hands once in agreement and bowed her head.

"As the goddess wishes," she said respectfully.

"Good. I will heal your child, but first, we must tend to this other matter. The stars that guide me are traveling this way, and this spell is at its most potent under the sign of the bear."

"What is this spell, Astora?"

Although she had the courage to ask me, I did not feel compelled to tell her. I merely smiled. I could feel the woman's excitement at being included in Ahurani's work. We were sisters even though I barely knew her, sisters serving our goddess. Ahurani was a goddess of water and healing, but we kept her name quiet here, for many feared her and her husband, Ahurani Mazda. I am glad they feared her, for that meant they would fear me too.

"We will have to tie her down, I am sure of it. She is a fighter. I can tell by the look of her. Does she know nothing of our goddess?" I scolded her.

"Yes, she is a fighter. I have not trained her in our ways, priestess," Mareta replied in the secret language. I could hear her thoughts...*for I barely know them myself.* If I survived this and returned to Zerzura, I would have to remedy that.

I could see the curious girl cast a fearful eye over my knife and bowl. In a flash, Mareta clapped the girl's mouth shut with her hand as I lifted the child's small body up and placed it on the pallet. Vainly she kicked and twisted.

"If you were wise," I said in a low whisper, "you would not fight this, Ziza. Today, you serve the goddess of your mother. This is an honor only a few get to enjoy." But Ziza did not stop screaming, and Mareta continued to muffle her cries. She whispered to her, trying to calm her, but her daughter saw the knife and feared it.

"I am going to take your blood, Ziza, but not all of it. The goddess does not require your life today. Your blood is precious to her. It is sweet and innocent, a fitting offering for this work." Expertly, I tied her feet and hands together with the straps. She struggled as her mother clamped her hand harder over her mouth.

I could have been kind and numbed the area before I sliced it, but I did not. I took my curved blade and slid it into the plump flesh of the child's left palm, right where it curved to make the mound of Ahurani. Many did not know it, but this was the seat of power for the soul. I made a clean slice, and the girl screamed in panic. If I had cared to look, I would have seen her eyes full of tears. I did not. Did she think she was the first child to feel pain?

I pressed the wound with expert fingers and drained the blood into the bowl. Feeling victorious, I covered the jade bowl and slid it with its precious contents back into place in my cabinet. I would use it when I was done with this current task. "See? You are not dead." Mareta untied her daughter while I wrapped her hand with a clean bandage. As soon as she was free, the girl ran out of the house like a fool. Mareta called after her, but she did not answer or return. What did it matter? I did not care who she told now. I had what I wanted, the blood of an innocent. What could be more powerful for what I had in mind?

I quickly examined Mareta's sick child and sent the goddess-sister home, promising to send for her soon. The child had a climbing fever, but I assured her mother it was nothing serious. The child would not die. Once Mareta left me, I quickly forgot about the sick girl. I took the blood-filled bowl and searched for a quiet place where I could be alone under the stars. I remembered the abandoned courtyard that no one visited. I had half claimed it as my own, and it would be perfect for what I needed to do. I drew the sacred symbols in the sand and tossed the holy items into the center of the circle. Still holding the bowl, I fell on my knees and beseeched the goddess to send me to Egypt. "Send me," I pleaded with her. "My son needs his vengeance. Please do not doom him to dwell in darkness."

I raised the bowl above my head and removed the lid. In the holy language, I spoke the words of power and drank the bowl of blood. It was bitter and metallic, so I swallowed it quickly. I had not eaten in many days, and I thought I would vomit it up, but I did not. I lay on the ground in the circle and waited for the change to happen. I waited for Ahurani's response.

Again, I pleaded with her, "Take your revenge through me, goddess. I will defeat Egypt's queen for you! Let all fear you!" I whispered into the darkness. Even though my stomach felt sick and my head swam with grief, I waited, hoping to see the evidence of Ahurani's approval. I began to wonder if she refused me, but then I felt the change begin. My skin crackled and my bones hurt. In the darkness I stared at my hands and could see the skin smoothen. I now had smaller, younger-looking hands. The tattoos had disappeared! I lay still for a little longer, allowing the goddess to shape me how she wanted. I knew this had been her will! I had indeed heard her voice! She accepted me and approved my plans. Ah, but this was deep magic. What price would this cost me? In my excitement I pushed the fleeting worry away. This was a grand honor!

My body began to convulse, and pain shot through me like a dozen flaming arrows. I flailed under the weight of Ahurani's invisible hand until I passed out. Sometime later, I woke to see that the stars had moved in their courses significantly. I had slept for many hours, but now the process was complete. I scrambled to my feet and walked back to my white stone abode. I was so ready to see my new self in the mirror that I practically ran to my table. I stared into the gold-framed mirror. Moonlight bounced off the white stone outside my window and illuminated the room enough for me to see that I had truly changed. I was younger, fairer. I appeared a strange blend of Ziza and Astora, with no tattoos and extremely long hair. If I had to guess, I would say that I appeared to have seen a mere fifteen seasons. I was very pleasing to look upon. Yes, this incarnation would do quite well for the Egyptian court. Even Pharaoh would not be able to refuse me.

I immediately began to pack my bag. This illusion was a gift that would last only until the next full moon. Then I would be exposed for who I was—the wife of Omel, the true and rightful king of the Meshwesh. There was also another danger. Any person who truly knew me would not be fooled by this magic. I had to be careful to keep myself hidden until I was ready to reveal my true identity. Excited, I stuffed the rest of the items I needed in my bag, including the lovely robe with the enchantments woven into the stitches. Yes, time was my enemy, but I was determined to take vengeance for Suri. Even if it cost me my life, this was all that mattered.

I had forgotten the sick child who was still lying on my table. Setting my bag down for a moment, I retrieved the pouch of medicine I would use for the healing magic from my nearby cabinet. As I began to burn the herbs in the small silver brazier near the child's head, I noticed that she was not breathing. The breath of life had escaped her lips while I had waited on Ahurani, and she no longer dwelt in this realm. Perhaps the goddess had required more than I had imagined? Perhaps the bowl of blood had not been enough? This was unfortunate, yet I could not call her back. I touched her tentatively. Her body was cold and no longer a suitable host for her soul. I blew out the flame and walked out of the house. I had no time to tend to a dead body. Her mother would find her soon enough. At least she could claim her and send her to the Otherworld with the proper ceremonies. My son dwelled in darkness.

The girl had served her purpose, and now I must serve mine.

Chapter Two

B*right Horizon—Nefertiti*
Amenhotep and I spent another day exploring one another's bodies, stopping our mutual appreciation long enough to worship the Aten, eat a light meal, and perhaps soak in one of the refreshing pools in the palace. How easy it had been to lose myself in that discovery! I felt love, a deep, surprising love—one that I never expected. My husband declared that I would accompany him always and had even moved my belongings to his personal quarters. According to Menmet, my maidservant and confidante, this was never done.

"Even the Great Queen Tiye was not so honored," she told me with wide eyes. "Pharaoh loves you, there can be no doubt," she had whispered in my ear when I saw her briefly earlier that day. "I am sure he intends to make you his Great Wife. I am sure of it!"

"Do not say such things, Menmet. Not here."

She looked around suspiciously and then, seeing no one about, smiled confidently at me. "There are none of Tadukhipa's spies here. Only me." She bowed her head, and the tiny silver bells woven into her wig tinkled lightly. She was a petite young woman with a pretty face and a childlike voice. "However, I hear that those new dancers, the lovely ones with the yellow skin, are from her court."

"Yes, that is what I hear too, but I cannot refuse them. Help me find something to wear, please." Although it was foolish to think it, I felt by avoiding speaking of Tadukhipa or hearing her name, I might prolong my time with my husband a little longer. Amenhotep was not husband to just one woman, but for now, he was only mine.

This evening had been one of the few times I had left Amenhotep's side in the past few weeks. With Menmet's words ringing in my ears, we walked back to Pharaoh's apartments. He greeted me as if he had not seen me in a week, although we had been parted only less than a few hours ago.

He wrapped his strong arms around me and showed his broad smile. He now wore a robe of green with a gold scarab on the back. It had a wide golden ribbon stitched along the hem. I had never seen one so finely made. His head was bare, as it always was when we worshiped the Aten, yet even without his double crown, he looked every inch a king. He kissed my forehead and led me out into the courtyard, and side by side we walked up the stairs to view the Aten as it set on the far horizon, completing the day's journey. With a nod, he directed me to take my position, and I did as he instructed. As the Aten began to drop away, we worshiped with our hands and with our words until the Aten disappeared, leaving only the musky night and a few bright stars behind.

I slid my arm under his, and together we stood on the balcony overlooking Thebes. We were high above the city, which sprawled like a tangled cluster of fireflies below us. Life did not slow in Pharaoh's city after dark. This was not like living in the Red Lands. I laid my head upon his shoulder and closed my eyes. I must have been dreaming. Was this all a pleasant dream? We stood there in silence for a long while.

"Neferneferuaten. Do you know what that means?"

I smiled up at him proudly because I did know. "Perfect are the perfections of the Aten."

"It has a double meaning, my love. What else does it mean?"

I chewed my lip and searched my memory for an answer. My answer seemed important to him, and I did not want to disappoint. After a moment, I had to confess. "I do not know, husband. Please tell me."

He touched my lips with his finger and said, "Beautiful are the beauties of the Aten. That is why I named you such. You are a gift to me, from the Aten. A beautiful, perfect gift."

"Then I am happy indeed. Happy to be Neferneferuaten."

"Let us dine. I have invited the court to come and help us celebrate." I swallowed nervously at the thought of interacting with Amenhotep's court. I had few friends here, but since my official marriage, no one (including Tadukhipa) had openly spoken against me. He must have spotted my reticence, for he said, "As much as I would like it to be true, we cannot hide in our rooms forever."

"Yes, I know." I stood on my tiptoes and kissed him one last time before walking downstairs to the feasting rooms. "I am ready."

We walked down together in the formal way, my hand resting on top of his, our heads held high with a serious gaze, our eyes fixed on what was in front of us at all times. What had once felt unnatural and statuesque was natural to me now. Menmet had helped me practice my posture and movements, and I was thankful for her help.

Immediately the people below us began to bow and praise their Pharaoh. I followed Amenhotep's example, remaining aloof as we walked into the dining room. As this was an informal dinner, or as informal as a dinner could be at Pharaoh's court, we did not wait to be announced but sailed to our seats. Amenhotep and I took our place at the head of the table, and immediately cheerful music began to play. There were fewer than a hundred people in the long, decorated room, and many faces I had never seen before.

Some I had.

I recognized Ramose immediately. The rugged-looking general was the first to greet us. He kept his eyes trained on Pharaoh but showed me respect as well with a polite half-bow and a murmur of greeting. I was perfectly aware that Ramose was angry with me. Angry that I had not yet produced Ayn—and his long-awaited, highly desired child. Angry that his wife, Inhapi, had not yet been avenged. I sighed inwardly. This was a matter I could not avoid forever. Ayn would have to return and face her crime, if that was indeed what it was. I missed her and had hoped that Ramose would have changed his mind in this matter. My hope appeared to be in vain. I stood awkwardly, waiting for Ramose and Amenhotep to end their conversation. Instead, the two men walked away from the crowd for a few moments, probably to discuss some important matters regarding Pharaoh's recent foray into the southernmost areas of Temehu. Although he did not consult me in his military plans, I hoped his soldiers destroyed what remained of the Kiffians. I could easily conjure Gilme's face again. I would never forget his dying expression, so full of rage and lust was he. Then I remembered he was dead and would always be dead. That gave me a modicum of satisfaction. If only my sister and I could have killed him a hundred more times.

I greeted the string of well-wishers who walked past me with nods and waited patiently for the return of my husband. It took longer than I expected. After the general's departure, Amenhotep returned to my side, and many more courtiers came to stand before us. The seemingly endless crowd spoke kind words and bestowed their happy wishes on us. Behind us on the dais, scribes swiftly recorded the names of the visitors and made sundry other notes with their blackened quills and stacks of papyrus. I had learned quickly that nearly everything having to do with Pharaoh and his family got memorialized in some kind of record. It was an odd thing to get used to. I leaned back against my cushion and waited for the formalities to end.

All, including Ramose, offered us gifts of food, oils, silken fabrics, or gold. Nobody came before us empty-handed. I nodded when appropriate, but most of the courtiers seemed happy to speak only to Pharaoh, not to me. I felt no slight. That was a great relief. In some cases, Amenhotep would leave his seat and embrace the courtier or whisper something in his ear.

One young man, Karebi, came proudly before us and laid two boxes of incense on the low table that we reclined behind. I recognized him because he had visited the Court of the Royal Harem to wait upon Queen Tiye on several occasions. I thought we had spoken once, maybe twice, but I did not know him. Karebi had wisely waited until the majority of the attendees had completed their speeches before taking his place before our table. Better to be last and remembered, I could almost hear him thinking. I scolded myself for thinking such things, but that was the way it was here in Egypt. Someone was always clamoring for something. I now understood better why the Great Wife had become so sour on court life.

Karebi bowed low and waited for Pharaoh to acknowledge him. My stomach was growling, but I had to wait until everyone had a chance to speak before I could eat. In this, I would follow my husband.

"Karebi. Welcome back to my palace. You have words to speak?" I noticed Amenhotep's tone sounded slightly different with this young man than with the others. But as Karebi seemed not to notice, I thought not much of it either. Perhaps I was just hungry. Why hadn't I eaten while I was in my rooms earlier? Poor Menmet. I should have taken the fruit she offered me.

"My Pharaoh and my Queen. I have a poem to share with you, my lady, a poem of admiration and love." As this was the first courtier to speak to me directly, I purposefully kept my attention on his face and listened with great expectation.

"*She is one girl, but there is not another like her,*" Karebi began with a smile. He glanced at his young wife, who sat at one of the lower tables. I recognized her, although her name escaped me now, but I kept my respectful attention on the young man.

She is more beautiful than any other.
Look, she is a star goddess arising in Egypt
Just like the light that rises at the beginning of a happy new year.
Brilliantly white and bright-skinned is she,
with beautiful eyes for looking into my soul.

My cheeks turned red under my makeup, and I tried to ignore the giggling of Menmet and the others who thought Karebi's praise was a bit excessive. Neither he nor his wife seemed to notice, and he continued on.

"Oh, her lips, with sweet lips for speaking. She has not one phrase too many—"

Suddenly Amenhotep leaped from his chair, knocking it over backward as he stalked around the table. I too leaped to my feet, wondering what had happened. My husband's body language demonstrated that he was anything but relaxed. Karebi did not expect this reaction, and neither did I. I sat up rigidly and caught my breath. Everything went quiet, including the festive music and the laughter of my silly servants. My husband grabbed the startled Karebi by the arm and led the short man outside the banquet hall. So violent was Amenhotep's manner that I could not hide my look of surprise, even though Memre had trained me extensively on concealing emotions. What had happened?

Confused, I searched for Menmet's face in the crowd. She did not look at me. Her attention was on the courtyard beyond, and her hand flew to her mouth. I could not see for myself, but I heard someone scream in pain. Soon two of Pharaoh's guards jogged to the courtyard. Now everyone was gasping and whispering except the young man's wife, who was as white as the marble columns that lined the room. I was very near to calling Menmet to me when Amenhotep returned to the banquet hall. As he took his seat, one of his manservants stooped next to him, holding a bowl of water and a linen towel. Without a word, Amenhotep washed his hands, and I watched in shock as the water turned red with blood. Karebi did not return to the hall. In fact, his wife was now being escorted out by the two guards who had assisted Amenhotep in the courtyard.

As Pharaoh wiped his hands with the towel, he called, "Food!" I could see that his hand was bleeding, that it was not just Karebi's blood. I picked up a linen napkin, thinking to pat his wound, but Menmet touched my hand and shook her head discreetly.

As she pretended to adjust my wig, she whispered in my ear, "The blood of Pharaoh is sacred. Do not touch it, for it is a god's blood."

I stared at Amenhotep, wondering what to do. All of the court watched us and tried to determine for themselves what was amiss with the happy young couple.

My husband leaned toward me and whispered in my ear, "I will not share you, Nefertiti. Do not give me a reason to doubt you."

I took his hand and whispered back, "Never! What has happened? Tell me." Suddenly I worried. Had someone spoken to him about Alexio? It had been only infatuation; I could see that now. It had been only the hopeful dreams of a girl. Amenhotep was the one I loved. I could not explain the workings of my own heart. I had not expected these feelings or known the depth of them with Alexio, but it was the truth. "Please," I said, reaching for him as he pulled away. He left the banquet hall again, sending the court to whispering and pointing. I followed him, uncaring about protocol or anything else. I sensed that more hung in the balance than just my feelings. This was not a lovers' spat but an accusation. And one Amenhotep believed.

"Wait!" I called out to him. "My husband, what is the matter? I do not know this Karebi. I swear it!"

He raised a long finger in warning. "I will not share you! Not with anyone!" The intensity of his words and the fierceness of his eyes stunned me, but I felt compelled to soothe his suspicions. My mouth moved, but the words did not form. Amenhotep stood with his hands on his hips and stared at me as if I were a stranger. "Think carefully what you say to me, Nefertiti." He was warning me about something, but what? Everything had been fine between us until we came to dinner.

Until he spoke with Ramose.

As fearful as I was and as desperate as I felt, I could not let the general's accusation go unchallenged. It was true I would never have dreamed that I, Nefret hap Semkah, would ever love an Egyptian, much less Pharaoh. But that was before.

Suddenly, Tiye's words rang in my ear: *"You can live a prisoner, or you can become a true Queen."*

More than anything, I wanted to become Queen Nefertiti—Neferneferuaten, wife of Amenhotep, beloved of my husband and Pharaoh. With every fiber of my being, I wanted this. Egypt—no, Amenhotep—had woven a spell around me, but apparently it was a spell that seemingly could be easily broken.

"I have given you no reason to doubt my commitment to you. Although I am not an Egyptian, the Aten brought me to you, Amenhotep. I have been truthful with you in all things. I swear it on my life! There is no one but you, nor shall there ever be. You have no need to worry despite what others may say. I have not been unfaithful in word or deed." I felt a chill, and gooseflesh rose on my arms, but I did not move a muscle. I met his dark eyes with assurance and trust. He appeared to soften a little, but his manner was still guarded. I could not back down! "And I challenge anyone to say otherwise!" To show him how serious I was, I took his hand and kissed his bleeding wound fearlessly. Now he could kill me if he so chose, for I had touched the sacred blood. This was a test of his love, one that could cost me everything. "I swear it on your blood, my husband and Pharaoh. Let it testify against me if I speak a lie."

Ignoring the rising whispers in the banquet hall, the crowd nosily peered through the opening in the gauzy curtains, I continued to meet his gaze fearlessly. To think all my happiness, all our happiness, could be undone so quickly by a few words. Accepting my gesture at last, he kissed me and breathed a sigh of relief. "I should not have doubted you. I will not do it again."

"You will never have a reason to doubt me, Amenhotep. I am yours. Always." I gave him a confident smile and walked with him back to our dining table. As we settled back down to eat, I cast a warning glance in Ramose's direction. He smiled amusedly and lifted his cup to me, but I kept my face a mask—just as I had seen Pah do during the mekhma trials. Better to let him wonder what I was thinking than give him the satisfaction of seeing his handiwork achieve its goal. Although my husband's fears had been abated for the moment, it wounded me to think he would believe that I would betray him. My mind immediately began to dissect the situation. Inhapi had been Tadukhipa's great friend—and more, if you believed the rumors. Perhaps Ramose had scattered those seeds of distrust on her behalf? I would probably never know. All I could do was prepare for whatever came next.

I forced myself to put on a distant smile and pretend that I wanted to be in attendance. Thankfully there were no more formalities, and immediately the music picked up the notes of a happier song. Neatly dressed servants appeared with trays of decadent food offerings. Each came and stood before us with their temptations. They kept their eyes cast down and waited for Amenhotep's steward to dismiss them.

I had little appetite now, but Amenhotep poured wine into my cup. "Drink, this is not juniper wine," he said teasingly. Obediently I reached for the large silver cup, happy to hide my face behind it if only for a few seconds. I did not want him to see the sudden rush of tears pushing against my eyelids. As if she could read my mind, Menmet came to sit beside me again, and as the platters appeared before us, she dutifully filled my plate with the foods I normally liked to eat. She selected two duck eggs, along with fresh berries, dates, a half-pat of cheese, and the soft honey bread the Egyptians loved from the highest to the lowest. I too had begun to love the baked treats, but I longed for chula bread and the sweet waters of Timia. Those to me were the greatest food and drink one could ever have.

I ate timidly at first, but when I saw no one watched me or stared, I ate to my heart's content. This was the first meal Amenhotep and I had enjoyed outside our rooms in weeks. Now those days seemed like a dream. Tomorrow our honeymoon would officially end, and we would begin our life together in earnest. I suspected that I would see him less, but as long as we had some time together, I would be content. As he had many matters to attend to, so did I. I could turn my attention once again to my people. I needed an ally beyond my servants, but the idea of forgiving Omel filled me with revulsion. I worried over the fate of the Meshwesh. How did they fare in their new city? How was my father? Would he marry again? In my last message from Orba, I had heard that he might. I had not disapproved. A king needed a good wife, and I had no doubt that Leela loved my father. I wondered about Pah and Alexio but did not dare put any questions concerning them in writing. Surely if something were amiss, I would know it. And what could I do if there were problems?

I smiled at Amenhotep, who was sharing a joke with another of his closest confidantes, Saho the Prophet. Although Saho did not speak to me, even in greeting, at least he was not Ramose.

Menmet poured me another glass of wine and pointed to the new dancers who had arrived in the hall. These were the gifts sent to us from Tadukhipa. They wore splendid purple ribbons that covered their lithe bodies perfectly. They swayed and wound about the room, and their skin glistened as they paced through their synchronous movements. With upraised palms, they surprised us by adding subtle movements that were reminiscent of our Aten worship. I could see by his delighted smile that Amenhotep did not miss the intricate movements either. As the twelve dancers traveled the wide circle they came together in perfect timing, clapping their hands to accentuate the effect of their synchronized steps. The girls appeared remarkably alike. In fact, it was easy to believe they were related. As Menmet noted earlier, they had unusual yellow skin, probably made more unusual with paint, round bottoms, and tiny feet. Unlike the servants who brought us food and drink, the dancers met our eyes boldly and constantly wore smiles. I could see one in particular cast a lustful eye on Amenhotep as she waved her fingers in rhythm. He did not bother to hide his appreciation.

How amusing! He all but accuses me of unfaithfulness but does not mind staring at Tadukhipa's dancers. Farrah was right! Men's hearts are attached to their male parts and are easily handled—and stolen.

I took another sip of my wine. I could hardly believe it, but Karebi returned to the festivities. His smooth brown skin was marred by an ugly black bruise that encircled his eye. He appeared a humbled man. At least he was wise enough not to look at me or speak to anyone. He merely ate his food and sat staring at his plate. His wife did not return. Ashamed of her husband, no doubt. Well, at least he was alive. I knew it was not wise, but I felt some sympathy for the little man who reminded me of Orba. However, Karebi was not as wise as Orba. When the song ended, Karebi rose, and the dining hall hushed. He walked to the foot of the table again, but I pretended I did not see him. Menmet and I were admiring the golden fish that swam in a large blue glass bowl on the table. It was a beautiful gift from one of Pharaoh's courtiers.

"Watch this, Menmet. Give me some bread." I was tired, and the wine was making me lightheaded. I giggled with Menmet as we dropped the bread in the water and watched the greedy little fish come to eat it and stare at us, hoping for more.

She smiled and looked at me in surprise. "How wonderful! Look how hungry he is! You have hidden talents, my Queen. How did you learn this trick?"

"By accident. I was sitting under the palm tree with...with a friend, and we happened to toss our bread in the water. The fish came to the top and begged for more. After that, we could not make them go away. They love chula bread—and honey bread too, it seems."

"How smart you are!"

Karebi cleared his throat, and I turned my attention to him. My husband watched me as I acknowledged the wary courtier. "Karebi." I did not know what to say. I hardly knew what his original offense had been.

"My Queen, I beg your forgiveness for my inappropriate words."

He had not offended me. I had thought him only a silly man, but I would not go against my husband. I glanced at him, but Amenhotep offered me no guidance in this matter, and I did not seek his counsel. "You are forgiven, Karebi. Please enjoy your meal and send my regards to your wife."

With a sad expression, Karebi backed away from the table and slowly exited the building. Not many people paid much attention to him now. After seeing Pharaoh's wrath break out against him so savagely, I doubted if anyone wanted to offer their friendship to the foolish little man.

Suddenly Amenhotep rose from the table. "Goodnight to all of you. In the morning, Queen Nefertiti and I will rise to greet the Aten. You are all welcome to join us."

The courtiers applauded loudly and cheered. They seemed excited and even honored to be invited to worship the Aten with Pharaoh Amenhotep and his new wife. I rose and placed my hand on top of his. I smiled up at him, but his look was serious and reserved. My heart fell in my chest. I had done nothing to cause him to doubt me. Then it occurred to me that it must be very difficult to be the Pharaoh to wonder all the time who loved him and who was merely using him. I would never be that. I would never do that, no matter what! Amenhotep was an honorable man who wanted to bring his people into a new age, an age of enlightenment and religious freedom for Egypt.

He frequently said, "The people should be free to worship whom they choose! How can we dictate a man's conscience?" He was so passionate about this, it frightened me at times.

He knew the oppression the House of Amun laid on the people. There were times in the past when they demanded up to half of the income of the worshipers. Even Pharaoh was not immune from this taxation, for what else could you call it? I was honored that he chose me to be his Queen and partner in this great quest. Who was I that fate would snatch me up from my obscure tribe in the Red Lands and bring me here to be a Queen of Egypt?

As our courtiers applauded, Amenhotep and I walked out of the banquet hall. I thought my husband would invite me into his chambers, but he stopped outside the massive golden door.

"Will we not be together tonight?"

"No, I cannot. There are pressing matters that I cannot avoid any longer." He must have noticed my worried expression, for he touched my cheek with his hand and said, "All is well, Nefertiti."

"Very well." I blushed, embarrassed at his refusal. Would the yellow-skinned dancer be visiting my husband's room later? What was I doing? I could not become a jealous shrew! Amenhotep loved me—that I was sure of! I added, "My door is always open to you, my love. If I am asleep, wake me, but come to me if you can."

Amenhotep softened his expression and held me against his warm body. I could not help myself and kissed him quickly but did not prevent his departure. With a return kiss on my forehead, he left me, and I watched him walk away.

Menmet scampered beside me. "Do not be sad, my Queen. It is good to be apart, for when you come together again, there will be much passion. Much passion to be shared, and soon many, many babies. Pharaoh will want to have many, many children. Many sons and many daughters."

I laughed and said, "Please, Menmet. I have not had the first child yet, much less many sons or many daughters."

"Don't you want many sons and many daughters?"

"I want as many daughters and sons as the Shining Man will give me, but not all at once. I would like to spend some time getting to know my husband first."

"What is to know, my Queen? He is handsome and virile, and he loves you. How jealous he is of you!" She picked up the clothing I let fall to the ground and helped me remove the wig and the thick, heavy jewelry. Handing them to another servant, she began to brush out my long red hair with her clever fingers and helped me remove my makeup with scented cream.

I watched her as she worked on her tasks. She looked nothing like her father, Heby. I'd had a chance to see the man up close when he visited her a few days ago. She had not asked me to greet him, and I must admit I was relieved. The more I heard about him and the other priests, the less I liked him. They did not approve of me, I knew this much, just as they had not approved of Queen Tiye's marriage to my Amenhotep's father. Heby had left Menmet in tears, but she had refused to confide in me or reveal the reason for her misery. I could have commanded her, but I would not. Menmet was more of a friend than a servant. How much of a friend would I be if I compelled her to share her heart with me?

As I bathed, Menmet filled me in on the palace gossip. Aperel, the handsome Master of Horses, had finally taken a new wife. In her cheerful manner, she explained how many in Thebes thought he loved only his horses. But he had surprised everyone with his marriage to a young girl from the east. It was said she had blue eyes, the color of the sky. I pretended to listen as I bathed and as she dressed me. When I finally climbed into bed, I was exhausted. I thought I would stay up and listen to the musicians who played for me in the courtyard below, but I did not. Their seductive soft tunes put me to sleep quickly, and I entered the dream world where I found the Shining Man waiting. I ran toward him with my arms extended, and then suddenly...

I was standing at the Blue Altar again, where Amenhotep and I married. Perched above us atop the altar was the Shining Man. The wedding went just as I remembered, but in my dream, I could see silver cords—no, silver snakes—wrapping around the two of us as we held hands. Suddenly, the three of us were no longer at the Blue Altar but standing in a high place on a cliff that overlooked a large body of water. It was greater than any pool of water or even the sea. Amenhotep and I knelt before the Shining Man, and he placed shining crowns upon our heads. The crowns were illuminated—they shone like stars. These were crowns unlike any I had ever seen before. Suddenly, the gods of Egypt stood at the edges of the water. I could see Isis, Amun, Set, Hathor and a host of others. As we rose to stand with our crowns atop our heads, they fell on their faces before us. I gasped at the sight. The Shining Man said some words that warmed my heart, but when I woke up, I immediately forgot them.

And when I did wake, Amenhotep was there, smiling down at me in the dark.

"Who were you dreaming of, my love?"

Hearing his voice thrilled me to no end. "The Shining Man, husband. I saw him in all his glory. He gave us crowns and said words of power over us."

"Tell me the words. What were the words of power?" He lay beside me, moving the wild strands of hair from my face.

I hesitated. "I do not know. I can't remember, but I shall try harder next time."

"It is no matter. I am here now. I am not a dream." He slid into the silky sheets with me, and my wandering hands let me know that he had already shed his clothing. "Let us make an offering to the Shining Man and see if we can both have a dream," he said before he kissed me.

"I am in a dream now, surely. Kiss me, Amenhotep. Kiss me, my love."

We made love and then settled down to sleep. I did indeed dream about the Shining Man again, but when Amenhotep asked me the next day, I lied to him.

I could not tell him what I saw. It would break his heart.

It surely broke mine.

Chapter Three

L*ife of Trials—Nefertiti*
The priests of Amun, adorned with leopard skin capes, filled the court with the strong scent of their incense. If they thought that their surprise assemblage or their numbers would deter my husband from his not-so-secret plans to uproot their oppression, then they highly underestimated him. Amenhotep was not a man to be swayed by popular opinion. I was neither invited nor forbidden to sit with my husband for this meeting, which I had learned in the past few months of my queenship meant I could come or go at my pleasure.

Today, I chose to stand unseen behind the thick blue curtains that hung behind my husband's throne. He knew I was there and never betrayed my secret attendance. I was curious to hear how he ruled his kingdom. Perhaps one day, I would have to do the same. It was better to learn the ways of court from one who understood its deep workings, someone who knew the traditions and expectations of the people who came before him. Menmet stood anxiously beside me and giggled as she peeked through the tiny hole in the veil. Fortunately, the processional was so loud nobody could hear her. Not yet, anyway.

"I will send you away. Now quiet, Menmet!" I threatened her in a whisper.

"As you say, my Queen."

I dropped my voice now as the room began to settle. "Shush...and don't say another word, not even, 'as you say, my Queen.'" She frowned at me. For the fifth time today, I missed Ayn. At least with the warrior, I did not have to worry about her speaking out of turn.

Ayn, where did you disappear to?

I had sent numerous couriers to Zerzura to ask about her, but nobody knew where she was hiding. I wondered if perhaps Ramose had murdered my friend, hidden her body, and only pretended not to know her whereabouts. It would be an easy thing to do. Surely her child had been born by now! I had no news to pass on to the general or to the officials who demanded her arrest and conviction. I wondered how long they would tolerate my evasion.

Peeking through the veil, I could see the face of the rugged-looking general in the audience. Many Egyptian women dreamed of a marriage with such a man, but they did not know him as I did. He was cold, callous—more beast than man. He stood to the left of the throne and watched the proceedings with a clenched jaw. I studied him, remembering the bruises he left on my arms when he thought to take me at Zerzura.

Oh, yes, Ramose. My mortal enemy.

My husband's voice rang out in the court, "My brother priests of Amun and Re, I greet you as a brother, for have I not worshiped in the temples alongside each of you? Is this why you have come to me today? Are you here unbidden to upbraid me for my worship of the Aten? Surely you can see that Amun has nothing to fear from the Aten or from me."

"No, Pharaoh. You are as a god to us. You may do what pleases you. However, the people have stopped worshiping Amun. Our storehouses are empty, and the priests are starving."

Starving? Not a man appeared as if he had missed a meal. Even the youngest priests were rich men, or so I had heard, and enjoyed every lavish benefit accorded to them.

"A god, you say?" Amenhotep boomed. I knew he did not appreciate the comparison. Unlike his father, he did not think himself a god and, in fact, considered the thought blasphemous. "Where is your leader today? Maya, step forward."

"Here I am, Pharaoh."

"Tell me more about this problem that has driven so many leopard coats into my court today. It must be a serious matter to see so many faces assembled here before their Pharaoh."

I tried to count them all but gave up. There must have been several hundred all crowded into the court with stern expressions. It would not matter. They could assemble a thousand dissenters—it would not sway Pharaoh. Amenhotep's guard shuffled anxiously at the tone of his speech. Obviously, none of these men had witnessed Karebi's thrashing or heard the rumor that Karebi's wife had disappeared into the workhouses. I shivered at the idea that my husband had ordered such a punishment. I had heard of these workhouses but knew little about them except that they were not places to visit or to ask about.

Some of the priests could see that Pharaoh was not pleased with their unannounced visit to his court. Maya quickly continued with his calm reasoning, "Oh, Majestic One, I mean no disrespect. We come to you because only you can help us. The people are not bringing offerings to the temples—they are tempting the wrath of Amun!" I could hear the onlookers, the courtiers who regularly attended Amenhotep, whisper fearfully. The priest's words gripped their hearts with fear. Feeling empowered, I supposed, Maya continued on, "Just today we received less than half the normal weight in gold and food. And the people...they see their Pharaoh worshiping before the Aten—he no longer visits the temples. The people do as they see the Lord of the Two Lands do. Whatever your intention, it is clear that the support for the Aten has been to the detriment of those who serve Amun. Please tell the people to return to the temples! It is not wise to anger Amun in this way, Majesty."

Amenhotep stood, jumping up quickly as he had the night Karebi offended him. He paced the dais like a lion, a proud lion about to be sheared before his pride. Finally, he stopped and faced the crowd of men with their painted faces and their arms glittering with gold bracelets. "Who am I to tell Egyptians whom to worship? Some worship this one, some that one. It has always been this way. You want me to command the consciences of free men and women? In Egypt, even the slaves worship whomever they like. If your god has fallen out of favor, perhaps you should ask him why instead of coming to me to command the worshippers' obedience."

Maya stood blinking in surprise. "You are Pharaoh! We cannot command them, but you can. Is it not the place of kings to keep order in the kingdom? To instruct the people? We fear your silence in this matter will be misinterpreted as liberty to abandon our gods. Pharaoh must speak and remind the people of their duty to Amun!"

"You dare?" His voice rose sharply. "I well know my duty, Maya, as my father did before me. Blood has already flowed on behalf of Amun. Is he not yet satisfied?" The gathered men did not answer. That was wise. I held my breath as I watched. Menmet took my hand, and I felt her shaking beside me. Poor girl. Yes, I could see Heby in the crowd. How shameful to have such a father!

"What do you mean, my lord?"

"You know very well what I mean, Maya." I was sure the blood he spoke of belonged to his brother. It was an unspoken truth that the priests of Amun had no love for the sons of Tiye. I felt a chill as I wondered what they would think of my children. The children of Amenhotep and the Desert Queen.

In a sudden reversal of mood, Amenhotep waved his hand dismissively and said, "Nevertheless, I see that I have been shortsighted in this. It is not *my* desire to see blood spilled. Where is my scribe? Anai! Come!"

The tall, silent man shuffled forward and sat on the floor at Amenhotep's feet. He stretched out a papyrus and held a feathered pen.

"Send a letter to all of Thebes. Tell the people...tell them that we cannot forget our traditions. We must honor Amun with offerings. On behalf of Maya, I command the people to bring a fifth of this month's earnings to the temples of Amun."

"A fifth? That is too much, Pharaoh. We come only for what is due—no more."

Amenhotep smiled at Maya and said, "I am sure you will get what is due to you, High Priest. Leave now...with my blessing, of course."

I chewed my lip nervously as the priests began to exit the court in complete silence. I did not know what they hoped to achieve, but I was certain this was not it. The anger of the people would rise against them, I hoped. I prayed it did not turn against Amenhotep. As the court emptied, new petitioners entered, foreigners by the look of them. I wondered if these were the Hittites, Tadukhipa's people. I decided I had seen enough. I did not envy my husband.

Menmet whispered, "You saw my father? I am so ashamed. He thinks of nothing but those offerings. The priests are angry because the people support their Pharaoh! If he says the Aten is the supreme deity, then they listen. There is nothing these priests can do to stop that. Not even my father."

"I pray it does not go against our Pharaoh."

"The people will know that the priests of Amun requested this special offering." She pursed her thin lips in a thoughtful expression. Menmet had been snooping for me—there were problems in the kingdom. But weren't there always?

The late Amenhotep had made many promises and pledges to his old enemies, and a few foreign kings had sealed their deals with the Hawk of Egypt, as my father-in-law was known, with marriages. Many marriages. Some were official, and others were superficial unions arranged to bring special recognition to whatever dignitaries were in favor at that moment. Recently, I learned from my very knowledgeable Menmet that my Amenhotep was required to keep those wives in a place of honor even after his father traveled to the Otherworld. Amenhotep had inherited all the concubines of the Royal Harem, as was tradition, but the matter of queens and their management was handled quite differently in Egypt.

To make matters tenser, the Hittites were keen to establish their prized princess as the new superior queen and consort. They wanted to see firsthand how well their daughter, Tadukhipa, was being treated by this new dignitary. In fact, Menmet told me in a whisper late last night, they wanted Tadukhipa to be the Great Wife above everyone. I quietly vowed to myself that if she were to achieve that, I would run myself through with a sword. I would never live under her leadership. From the few times we had interacted, I knew for sure that she would kill me with a thousand slow deaths before she ever did the actual killing. Still, it was treasonous for me to bring accusations against any of the queens, as they were the wives of Pharaoh, so we did not speak about it any further.

When we returned to my chambers, I was surprised to see Memre waiting for me. I asked, "Lady, what are you doing here? Is everything well with Queen Tiye?" Memre licked her dry lips, and I added, "Forgive me. You must be thirsty." The old lady had a healthy appreciation for wine, so I filled a goblet, handed it to her, and waved Menmet away.

"Lady queen, Amenhotep's mother, the Great Wife of the late Pharaoh, has sent me to you. She wanted you to know that your sister is in the Green Temple of Isis near here."

Puzzled, I tilted my head and asked, "Sitamen, you mean?"

"No, Queen Nefertiti. I mean your true Meshwesh sister."

"You must be mistaken. She is not in Thebes."

"She is in the Green Temple. I have just come from there, and I saw her with my own two eyes, just as my queen bade me."

My hands flew to my chest, and I couldn't hide my shock. "Who would do this? I cannot imagine that she brought herself here."

Memre drained the cup and set it down on the table. I filled it again, hoping she would quickly tell me everything she knew. This was not likely. Memre was a careful woman, much like her mistress, and she would weigh her words before she spoke them. With a grim smile of thanks, she continued, "This was not done by the Great Queen's order, if that is what you are thinking. Forgive me, this was not Queen Tiye's order. She just heard it herself."

"What did Pah say? Did you speak to her?"

"The priestess who cares for your sister would not let me interview her. The girl is in seclusion until the new moon rises next week. The priestess, Magg is her name, says she is there to serve the goddess Isis. We will have to wait until then." Her eyes narrowed, and she stared into the cup thoughtfully. "But we know who ordered her installation in the Green Temple."

"Tadukhipa! But why?"

"We can only wait and see, but you can be assured that you have a stone enemy with the Monkey. She will never forgive you for stealing Amenhotep's heart or for the death of her friend."

"I had nothing to do with either of those things. I cannot command a man's heart. Would she harm my sister just to spite me?"

She nodded slowly, her eyes angry, and her mouth a red slit. "She will be much more careful than that. Kill her outright? No. But if she can bring you embarrassment with your sister's presence, why wouldn't she?"

With Pah out of her head, wounded to the soul by the Kiffians, there was no doubt that would be quite easy to accomplish. Memre continued, "Whatever Kiya's designs, it can only be for your sister's harm—and yours. Do not think Tadukhipa is going to lie down without a fight while you are made the Great Queen of Upper and Lower Egypt. She already endured that with Tiye. She does not like being second and has no desire to land in that spot again. She has determined to fight you for that right, and with the Hittites arriving soon, she will have the political persuasion she needs to accomplish her goal."

"My husband will never raise her above me. He would never do that."

Memre laughed. "Ah, but he's her husband too, isn't he? And he is Pharaoh and a man—and his father's son. His heart will not rule his head in this matter."

"In name only is he her husband!" I said defensively. "He does not love her, Memre."

"Love?" She snorted derisively. "We are not talking about love, Queen Nefertiti. We are talking about kingdoms and alliances and matters of state beyond your feelings, girl. I thought a Desert Queen would know this already. Love is a luxury reserved for bakers, brewers, and farmers—not for kings. Which brings me to the Queen's instructions..."

I knew what she said was true. I was no fool. Deep down, I had always known but had allowed myself to be swept up in the magic of Egypt and, in doing so, had lost control of my own heart. I had forgotten the reality of my situation. I sank into my chair, feeling deflated. The truth was I was here only because Queen Tiye put me here. With the old queen losing influence with her son as other advisers moved in, advisers like Ramose, it would fall upon me to secure my position as queen at his side. I could take nothing for granted. Especially a man's heart.

"What does Queen Tiye instruct, Memre?"

She whispered, "You know my queen hates Tadukhipa above all others. She reminds you of what she has done for you. You were an insignificant Desert Queen with no home and no army when she met you. Because of her favor, you are where you are now. It is time to get your head out of the clouds and think like a queen—a queen who wants to remain a queen. Queen Tiye orders you to make peace with your uncle. You need an ally. Lift him up with accolades, gifts and whatever honors are necessary. Send him home to rule for a time. Have him return with something of significance, and then offer this to the king on behalf of your people. In matters of wealth, you likely cannot match the Hittites, but your people can win by proving their loyalty to a greater degree. Prove to your husband and all Egypt that you are more than a peasant queen—more than a pretty face! Begin honoring Isis in public. Claim her as your mother often and loudly. I hear that you have never been to the temple. The Queen knows her son worships the Aten, but you must be careful to honor Isis and be seen doing so."

I clamped my mouth shut at the veiled insults and accepted the scolding. This was Tiye's way, and these were her words. "What else?" I asked.

"In a few weeks, a group of ambassadors from Grecia will arrive in Pharaoh's court. Although you are Isis' daughter now, it is appropriate for you to greet the Grecian delegates as kinfolk. Queen Tiye says you should do whatever it takes to make an alliance with Grecia. Whatever it takes, Desert Queen! Now is the time to build a following and make some alliances of your own. Fill your personal court with royalty, daughters who will be indebted to you and serve you. If you do not act now, you might as well pack your bags and move into the Royal Harem. Even now it might be too late."

"I see," I said as I tried to process the tasks presented to me. Could she be right? Was I in danger of being supplanted? Why must there always be competition in my life? I had not asked for this life of trials, and I had no idea how to change it.

"It would also benefit you to have an ally among the queens. Tiye is Pharaoh's mother, and Tadukhipa is your enemy, so it must be someone else. In her day, Tiye chose Tadukhipa as second wife, not because she loved her, but because she was wise."

I snorted in disgust. "Are you suggesting that I endorse Tadukhipa as second wife and hope she returns the favor?"

"No, that is not the way. Look to the other queens or someone else." She gave me a knowing smile.

"You obviously have someone in mind, Memre. Please tell me."

"I am speaking of Ipy." I waited for her to explain, but she pursed her lips and stared at me as if I were stupid. "You never heard of Ipy?"

"No, should I have?"

"Yes, I would think so. It is her crown you are wearing, lady queen. Ipy held Amenhotep's heart in her hands once, but her father stole her chances when he betrayed the old king. Forbidden to marry her, Amenhotep moved her to the Royal Harem, and that is where she has been ever since. He visits her from time to time, but not like he used to. Still, she might make a good ally against Tadukhipa. She hates her also."

"Why has he never mentioned her to me?"

"Should he? Have you told the king about your lovers? Anyway, it is old news now. She has never given him any children, and I think he's grown tired of her. If you were to invite her to court from time to time, she would no doubt be in your debt. Remember how lonely it is there? She is young and has no chance at life beyond the harem."

"That seems counterproductive, Memre. Why should I invite another rival to join me?"

"She isn't your rival. Ipy is a concubine with no hope of ever becoming queen. It is the law. A small kindness from you occasionally, like an invitation to dinner, would go a long way in increasing your status at the harem. Go see her when you can."

"Very well, I will do that."

"Oh, yes, there is one more thing."

"Another thing?"

"Yes, and this is more important than all the others..." she began slowly, "but I think you may have already accomplished this task." She grabbed my hands and stared at my palms for a few moments, and then cupped my chin with her right hand as she peered into my eyes. The speed of her movements surprised me, and I did not fight her. I stared back into her piercing eyes. The kohl rings around them were messy, and I could easily see a collection of fine lines. Memre was old—older than even Queen Tiye. A light breeze began to blow through the room, moving through the gauzy curtains and causing the green leaves of the potted palms to flutter. She chuckled and said, "You are pregnant, Queen Nefertiti. Pharaoh has planted his seed in your belly." She pointed her finger at me approvingly. "That is good. That will work in your favor. That is a thing that Tadukhipa has not yet achieved. Yes, the queen will be pleased."

"How do you know I am with child?" I could not hide my surprise.

She fell back in the chair and smiled at me. "You have much to learn about the ways of women, my Queen. Perhaps it is not your fault since you had no mother—no mother except Isis, that is. Call the physician, if you like, and have him examine you. You will see I speak the truth."

"I do not doubt you, Memre," I said with an embarrassed smile. Eager to come out from under her scrutinizing gaze, I rose from my chair and walked to the window to catch my breath and get some air. I watched the activity in the courtyard below. Many people, Egyptians and foreigners, streamed in and out of the court. The place seemed livelier than normal. I could feel the excitement in the air. Queen Tiye was right. I could not sit idly by and hope that Amenhotep chose me as his Great Royal Wife. I had my child to think about. "Please tell Queen Tiye I will do as she commands. I have no intention of bowing down to Tadukhipa."

Memre walked to the window and stood beside me. Patting my shoulder kindly, she said quietly, "Queen Tiye says to give you this greeting. She says you will know what it means." I pulled my attention from the window and watched in surprise as Memre made the Meshwesh sign of respect and said, "Hafa-nu, Queen Nefertiti." Tears flooded my eyes, and a sob escaped my lips. This was a sign that all would be well. I was not alone.

I returned the gesture and hugged Memre. "Hafa-nu, Queen Tiye. And Hafa-nu, Memre."

I turned my attention back to the window as the older woman left to return to her mistress. I watched Amenhotep as he climbed up on one of his new horses. It was taller than any horse I had ever seen, with a long, curved neck and strong, stocky legs. Amenhotep laughed as the animal pitched once and Aperel reached for the reins. I smiled at the sight. Leaning against the cold marble, I twisted a strand of my wig and enjoyed the moment. If Memre was correct, I would give my husband a greater gift than any horse or treasure.

I would give him a son. The breeze returned, and I heard a whisper. A familiar whisper. I had heard it before in my dreams.

Smenkhkare!

Chapter Four

The Heart of a Beast—Ramose

"Brother! What are you doing sitting alone in the dark?" Kafta asked me. His voice always sounded like a man who had been hanged but had escaped seconds before death. He waved the oil lamp at the darkness and lit the larger lamp on the table beside me.

"Who says I am alone?" I replied, tilting the jug upside down and draining the remnants of the sour liquid. It was meru, a stale workman's beer that I usually only drank when traveling with my men. I threw the jug down, sending shards of clay scattering around the room. The chained cat screamed in anger, and Kafta nearly dropped the lamp as he dashed out of its way.

"Gods! Why is that animal in here?" The cat's scream had sent the muscled man to the top of the table.

Any other time I would have laughed at the sight, but this was no laughing matter. "Come down from there. She cannot reach you. She is on a chain."

"I see that, but I do not trust chains."

At that, I did laugh. "But you trust exploding barrels of fire? You are a strange man, Kafta."

"I am strange? I am not sitting in the dark, getting drunk with a panther. Or is that a leopard? I do not care for cats."

"This is a panther. She belonged to Inhapi."

Kafta eased down from the table but stood no closer. "Come, brother. Let us go out to get some air. I see you drank all the meru. I have wine with me in my things. Come."

I stared bleary-eyed at the cat and then at Kafta. My eyes had grown used to the darkness. How long had I been sitting here? I could not remember, but it had been bright and sunny when I entered the animal's prison. The cat screamed again, and I yelled back at her as if I were a beast. She began to pace her side of the room, and her cold eyes never left me. They were dark and shiny—like the eyes of my dead wife. I had seen hundreds of dead men, but the sight of Inhapi's lifeless body lying on the priest's table filled me with unexpected dread. Now that I had lost her, it was easy to recall the few happy times we shared. How proud I had been to claim her as my own. She had been beautiful and welcoming, at least when we first married. As I traveled, she became less welcoming, but how could I blame her?

Inhapi had been shallow and silly at times, but she had put my name and my needs above everything else, mostly, and she worked tirelessly to see me elevated. She had not excited me as Ayn had, but she had been my partner in all things. I had betrayed her with the Meshwesh woman, and now Inhapi and my son were gone. It was true that Inhapi loved Tadukhipa, in ways I did not understand, but I knew that she had loved me too. Together we would see our names immortalized and find a place of prominence in this world and the next.

"Inhapi," I said, reaching my hand out to the cat's head.

"Stop that, fool! That cat is not your wife. You are indeed drunk, Ramose. Come, General of Egypt, before that animal tears into your hand. I can see she has not fed in a day or two. What are you trying to do? Feed yourself to the panther?"

With a grunt, he snatched me up, a thing he would never have done if I had been sober. I followed him outside, cursing him under my breath, but the cool evening air did feel good on my skin. "I have a message to deliver, but I will not do so while you are out of your head—and smelling like a beast." He led me to a trough of water. I didn't remember ordering a bath, but before I knew it, I was falling in. I sputtered and cursed as Kafta laughed. I was too drunk to climb out. All I could do was sit in the trough and yell at him.

"Now, now, General. Why make such a fuss? Wash, and I'll set you a meal. I see there are no servants here now. Did you send them all away?" He spotted my houseboy, Axteris, and yelled for him. As he gave instructions to the boy, I managed to climb out of the trough and struggled to remove my clothing. The cold water had sobered me up some, but not as much as I would have liked. Soon Axteris had my bath prepared, and I followed him to clean myself properly. Kafta followed me, chewing on bread and some kind of roasted meat. I reached for the soap and a sponge and went to work. I rubbed my face with my wet hand, feeling the stubble on my chin. How long had it been since I shaved? Or bathed? Or eaten? Lost in my grief for Inhapi, I had lost all sense of time. I had been in a place of forgetting. Now my friend, likely my only friend, Kafta was calling me back to life. I knew I should be grateful, but at the moment, I felt anything but gratitude.

The more I washed, the more I felt myself. What had I been thinking, climbing into that animal's hovel? Was Kafta right? Did I have a death wish? I was a man of strategy and reason, but I had no understanding or reasoning for what I had been experiencing. It was as if someone had cast a spell on me. As if I were walking under a shadow of doom.

"How long has Inhapi been dead, Kafta?" I asked him as he poured another pail of hot water into the tub.

With a surprised expression, he answered, "Almost two months, General."

"Two months..." I scrubbed my head with the soapy sponge and thought about the months that had passed so quickly. "The last thing I clearly remember is the night of Amenhotep's wedding party. Is it possible Queen Nefertiti poisoned me?"

He made a dismissive sound and tossed the bone he'd been gnawing onto a nearby platter. "You know the Desert Queen is not cunning enough to do something like that. I think there is a much simpler explanation for what has happened to you."

"What is it? Sorcery? Magic?"

"No, my friend." He sat on the edge of the tub and said, "It is grief. Grief can bring a man low, low enough even to wish for death. Low enough to make him play dangerous games with wild animals. The loss of Inhapi brought you low, but now you have a second chance at life. And you have the greatest reason of all to live."

"Really? What would that be? Some new battle? I have not heard anything from Pharaoh." I tried not to sneer. I remembered what it was like to be a new husband. Without waiting for an answer, I slid under the water. I held my breath and closed my eyes, pretending for a moment that I was dead. I would allow no air to pass through my body. My chest would not rise or fall. I could stay under this water and die. Inhapi would welcome me! In death, there would be no Tadukhipa or Ayn to come between us. She would be mine completely. As much as my mind commanded it, my body struggled, and my heart would not stop pumping. My ka refused to leave.

I rose from the water with a scream of anger on my lips. "Curse you, Osiris!" I shouted at the top of my lungs. Kafta jumped back and made the sign against curses. He was a superstitious man. "I cannot even die! The gods hate me, brother!"

"No, do not say that, Ramose. You are the General of Egypt and the servant of Pharaoh Amenhotep, although I must admit that seeing you taking a bath does not make for such an amazing impression. Get dressed now. We have much to talk about, preferably with your clothing on."

"I do not wish to talk."

"You will," he said. "The queen wants to speak to you. She has something that belongs to you." Kafta grinned, exposing the grand gap in his teeth.

I rubbed the water out of my eyes and blinked the rest away. "Who are you talking about? Nefertiti?"

"No, not the Desert Queen. Queen Sitamen wishes to speak to you."

Accepting the razor from Kafta, I began to scrape the hair off my face. My hands were so shaky I could imagine cutting my own throat without even trying. That might be the remedy to all my problems. I sneered at the idea of meeting with the spoiled, sulking princess. Although I had loved her father as my own, I had barely spoken to the girl over the years. I had been present during her "marriage" ceremony to her father, but so had most of the court. She was not overtly attractive, and I never gave her a second look. She was Pharaoh's daughter, not just any noble's daughter. When I was a younger man, I believed perhaps she admired me. Women often admire strength in men, and I had been a strong man—once. "What could the girl have to say to me?"

"She is hardly a girl, in case you haven't noticed," he said somewhat lewdly. "She has a gift for you."

"Well, what is it, Kafta, since you seem to know more than I? You seem bursting to tell me something."

In a deep, steady voice, he said, "She has your son, Ramose."

I stood naked in the tub, dropping the blade into the water. "What? Do not toy with me!"

"She has your son."

Stepping out of the tub, I yelled for Axteris. The young man returned with fresh linen towels. He immediately began drying my body. I could hardly believe my ears. "How do you know this is true? Did you see him?"

"Yes, it is the truth. I made her show me the boy herself. He is good-looking but small. Then again, I hear babies are generally small. They can't all be coming out of their mothers walking and talking like you and me." Kafta poured me a glass of wine mixed with water. "Here, you look like you need this."

I drank it and sat down in a padded chair as Axteris rubbed oil on my feet and wrapped a linen towel around my waist. "Tell me everything. I want to know everything."

"Sitamen did not confide in me about the details, General. I do not know how she managed it, but it is true. She has your son. Rescued him, I think. She wants you to come in the morning. 'Tell him to come and see his son,' she said to me in that voice of hers. You know it drives me mad."

Again, I ignored his insinuations. Sitamen was very childlike in many ways, including her voice. That was a trait that Kafta often enjoyed in women. "What of Ayn? Was she there too? Did you see her?"

"No, I did not."

"I see. Where is Sitamen, then?"

"At her new palace. She has left the Royal Harem for good, apparently. Some falling out with her mother. That is where we will meet her. If you are up to it?"

"Let us go now. I want to see my son."

"It is only a short ride. If we arrive before the appointed time, they may not let us in. You know how these royals are, Ramose. Best stick to the plan."

"Then we will sleep in our saddles, but I am going to see my son."

"Have it your way, Stubborn One. If you want to see the queen and your son looking like one of Osiris' dead army, be my guest."

A chill crawled up my spine. I scowled and said, "I don't look that bad."

"Yes, you do. But at least you smell better than you did." He grinned, showing his missing teeth. "Have patience and wait. Tomorrow will come. It always does! Unless you are dead."

"I was never any good at waiting."

He laughed again and nodded. "That is true. What will you name your son?"

I thought about Inhapi again. She had chosen the boy's name, so sure was she that Ayn would agree to our offer. "Kames will be his name." Weariness washed over me like an invisible force. I could not remember feeling more tired, even after a long campaign.

"A good name, General. Child of the bull, eh? Yes, that is a good name."

Suddenly, the black cat roared from her confinement. I had forgotten her. Maybe Kafta was right. I should stay at home one more night. I had some things to tend to anyway. "We will stay tonight and leave at first light."

"In that case, may I claim an empty bed?"

"Yes, the boy will show you where you can sleep. I will eat some food and sleep for a few hours myself."

"Very well, General." He left me alone to dress and sent Axteris away.

I could not help but think about my sudden change in fortune. The gods were not through with me after all. My son, he who would carry my name, was alive! As I shaved the last of the unwanted hair from my face, I thought about the cat. I walked to my rooms and retrieved my short sword. The cat screamed again as if she knew what I had planned.

When I entered her dank room, she met me with a low, menacing growl and swiped a wide paw at me. Silently I reached for the chain. Her dark fur was almost blue. Her eyes grew larger and brimmed with hatred as if she too blamed me for Inhapi's death.

"I promised you that either you or I would die, Evil One. You accuse me with your eyes, but I have done nothing. I did not know what Inhapi intended, nor did I bid her do what she did. Now, I intend to keep my promise. My son is alive, and my purpose continues. Yours, however, has come to an end."

Snarling deeply, she seemed to understand my meaning. I tugged the chain, pulling the cat closer to me as I wrapped the chain around my hand. She was close now, so close that she could assault me easily, just as I could assault her. I raised my knife above my head, gripping the handle expertly in my right hand as I prepared to make my move. We paced around the smelly room until she paused and I knew she was ready to take action. I snatched the chain as the cat pounced, sending her to the ground in a heavy thud. I had only a fraction of a second to deliver my blow, and I did it as if the gods themselves directed my hand. The panther's right paw came toward me again, and the claws gleamed as she extended them fully. Her aim landed, and she scratched me across my chest. I drove the knife into her chest as she screamed once and collapsed on the ground in a lifeless heap of fur and blood. After a few seconds, she stopped breathing and surrendered to her fate.

With one strike, I had killed the animal. I drove the blade into the heart of the beast.

I prayed this was a sign of things to come.

Chapter Five

The Aten—Nefertiti

The Aten dove under the far horizon, and Amenhotep and I shed our clothing and slid into the Crescent Pool. I swam deep into the cool darkness and bobbed to the top, kicking my feet as I rose to the surface with a smooth splash. He laughed in delight as I turned to dive again, unashamedly displaying my nude body for him. He dove after me and we swam down together, hiding from the world for a few seconds.

Here in the depths of the blue water, we were just Nefertiti and Amenhotep, two people who shared an unbreakable bond of love and purpose. Together we would build a new Egypt, a shining place full of love and peace. With a kiss we rose back to the surface, and soon we were frantically kissing and touching one another. I did not care that Pharaoh's guard, the Mazoi, lingered nearby.

Ever since the priests' unscheduled meeting in my husband's courts, tensions had grown in the Egyptian capital. Amenhotep had done as he promised and encouraged his citizens to give to Amun, but the order had the expected effect. The people took offense to the demand, but no one brought accusations against Amenhotep. As a result, more and more of the people, especially young men and women, abandoned the dark temples of Amun and joined us in worship under the open pavilions of the Aten. After each such ritual, whether it was the welcoming or sending away of the Aten, Amenhotep often talked with them, listening to their ideas and getting to know them. He was young—the crowds he drew were young. Together they were a force to be reckoned with. There was much excitement about this new time—the new age of the Aten.

And the priests were watching.

There had been rumors that some of the other temple priests and priestesses were unhappy too, but none were as vocal as those who represented Amun.

Amenhotep guided me to the side of the pool, and we made love under the stars. I whispered his name, as I knew he liked me to do, and wrapped my legs tighter around his waist. When we were through with our lovemaking, I floated on the water as he held my hands. I gazed at the stars above us. I never tired of looking at them, even though I saw them less often now. For a happy moment, I thought about Pah and how she used to point out each one with such excitement and how she would draw pictures with her fingers to show me the hidden shapes in the night sky. She had been so wise and kind when we were young girls. I had yet to go see her in the temple, but I had plans to do so tomorrow. I did not know what to expect.

"Come, Nefertiti. I cannot let you distract me any longer," he said with a soft smile. "I need to speak with you."

I swam toward him and climbed on his back, kissing him once more. "Is that what I am to you, a distraction?"

He smiled his wide, sexy smile but did not answer with a flirtatious comment as he normally would. As we stepped out of the water, servants ran toward us with clean linen sheets. They dried us, and I took my comb from Menmet's hand. She always seemed to snag my hair, because she had no hair of her own to contend with, I supposed. I had yet to shave my head like most Egyptian women of my status, and I had no plans to do so even though Menmet continued to advise me that I should. My husband loved my hair, and so far, I had not succumbed to the scourge of Thebes, brown lice. I had to admit there were times when the combination of my hair, a wig, and a crown made it unbearably hot, but my pride would not allow me to take the razor to my head. Not just yet.

I dressed quickly, and we sat at the small table. After combing the tangles from my hair, I handed the comb to Menmet. She sensed Pharaoh's mood and disappeared with the others. With a nervous glance, I could see them exiting the chambers together, something they rarely did.

"I have something to tell you."

"I too have something to share. But you go first, please." My heart was awash with excitement. The physician had left only a few hours ago, and he had confirmed Memre's expert appraisal. I was carrying Amenhotep's child. I could not believe I had waited this long to tell him my secret. "On second thought," I said quickly, "if I don't tell you now, I will burst! I have to tell you my good news."

Leaning on his elbow, his chin in his hand, Amenhotep gave me a permissive smile. I rose from my chair and stood before him, then suddenly knelt as a supplicant would. He said nothing, but I could tell by his stillness that my movement surprised him. I didn't know what he expected me to say, but I blurted out the words in a rush, "I am carrying your child, Pharaoh Amenhotep. It was confirmed by the physician this day."

When he didn't react the way I expected, I looked up cautiously. He walked away from me and began to pace the room, as he did when in deep thought or worry. I remained on my knees, worried about what he would say or do next. Without standing, I sat on the floor before his chair, my hand protectively over my still-flat stomach. Amenhotep paced and said, "This *is* a surprise, a complete surprise."

"A happy surprise?"

"What?" He paused his pacing and rubbing his chin.

I stood swiftly, angry and hurt. "You act as if I told you I stole some figs from the table. Didn't you hear me? I am pregnant, husband!"

"Of course I heard you!" Amenhotep walked toward me in three strides and put his hands gently on my shoulders. "This is the best gift anyone has ever given me, and I love you for it."

I hugged him impetuously, but I could sense that something was still wrong. "Then why is there no smile on my Pharaoh's face?"

"I am happy, but there is more to think about than just my happiness. Please sit, and I will tell you all." I eased into the chair and tossed my wet hair behind my shoulders. The silence was excruciating, but I waited to see what Amenhotep would say. "Years ago, my father entered into negotiations with several of our enemies. He was a man of peace, my father, despite what you might hear. He was not afraid of war, but he valued the blood of his people. He often said he would fight a thousand wars if the only blood that would spill would be that of our enemies."

He took a swig of wine from his cup and continued pacing. "At first the Babylonians and the Hittites refused his attempts at negotiations. But like so many others, they were too tempted by the gold of Kemet to resist. Eventually, they came to us, ready to parlay their way into an alliance. It was easy enough to do. Everyone wants Egyptian gold, but we laid heavy restrictions on our neighbors. By restricting the distribution of the gold to approved nations only, Pharaoh very easily brought the Hittites and Babylonians to Thebes."

Like a bolt of lightning striking a Benben stone, the full impact of his words began to reveal to me what this lesson in history was truly about. "This is about Tadukhipa, isn't it?" I swallowed, feeling miserable.

He didn't answer me directly, not at first. "It took work to bring them to their knees, but they eventually came to Thebes to submit themselves to Pharaoh. When they did, they were not humiliated. They were welcomed. Remember, the Hittites had been warring with us at that time for over twenty years. It was time to end the bloodshed. And yes, Tadukhipa's father was very eager to make peace, but one of the stipulations was that Pharaoh would take her into his household."

"I know this story," I said glumly.

"From whom? My mother? It is no secret that she hates Tadukhipa, and I suppose I would feel the same way if I were her. But Tadukhipa is not to blame. I am sure she did not ask to be traded for peace. However, that is only half the story. The Hittites expected to receive a bride in return, and the Hittite king wanted Sitamen. He was disappointed to learn that Egyptian kings do not simply give their daughters away. To make up for the perceived slight, Pharaoh promised to elevate Tadukhipa to the position of wife."

"Please just tell me what you want to say, husband."

"I cannot continue to ignore the wife I inherited, Nefertiti. The Hittites have come to see what I will do with Tadukhipa. I cannot send her back home in shame and risk a war between our nations."

"A war over one woman?"

He laughed bitterly. "Yes, and wars have occurred over much less. My advisers tell me this is no light matter. Can we risk such offense now when we are on the verge of a new kingdom? A new Egypt? I have the plans for our new city, a city dedicated to the Aten. Surely you see this."

"This has nothing to do with cities or the Aten! This has everything to do with us—Amenhotep and Nefertiti!" I was standing now, arms stiff and fists clenched.

"You think I want to do this? I sent my sister Sitamen away because I know she hates you. That was easy enough, but I cannot do that with Tadukhipa! She is a foreign king's daughter, and she was—is—the wife of Pharaoh! How now can she be anything less?"

I could not believe the words I was hearing. After all his talk of love and fidelity, Amenhotep was considering taking Tadukhipa as wife in the truest sense of that word, with all the privileges and experiences that came with that union. "I never asked you to send Sitamen away. We are not talking about your sister!"

"Tell me, my Queen. Have you never had to make a hard decision? Have you never had to go against your own heart? Is it so different in the Red Lands?"

I wanted to scream, "Yes, I have!" but I said nothing. I was afraid that if I opened my mouth, unintended words like, "I never wanted to come here!" would slip off my tongue. Or I might tell him the truth—he had not been my first love.

"This is nothing more than a formality. It will have no meaning at all, Nefertiti."

"A formality? When is lovemaking ever just a formality? Am I supposed to believe that will satisfy Tadukhipa? You and I both know what this is about!" This was about who would be his chief queen, the Great Wife of Egypt. Tadukhipa would do everything she could to convince him to raise her to that position.

"Yes, we do, and I must think about Egypt! I am, after all, Pharaoh!"

"Then think about Egypt!" If I could have stormed out, I would have, but doing so would have broken one of the rules of court. Never turn your back on Pharaoh unless dismissed. I could not deny it; Amenhotep had the upper hand. He always did. He always would. I could not afford to put myself in jeopardy right now. No more than I was at this very moment, arguing with the man who could order the killing of my entire tribe.

Amenhotep was furious at my lack of understanding. "When I first met you, I knew that I would love you, that you would be mine. I wanted you more than any woman I have ever met because you were strong, kind and intelligent. Not just for your beauty. Use that intelligence now, Nefertiti. Do you think I don't know how you must feel? I do know. I have spent my whole life doing things I did not want to do. This is just one more of those things."

My jealous heart resisted his reasoning. I did not want to forgive him or believe him. I did not want to accept what I must.

He continued, "The truth is, she is already my wife. I cannot now abandon her. Her uncle and cousins are here to observe my care for her. I do not need their approval, but I do not need war, either. Not when half the priests are against me! Is that what you want? Will that make you happy?"

"No," I said sullenly. "I do not want that."

Quietly, he said, "I do not think the arrival of the Hittites is a coincidence. Tadukhipa has complained to them, and now I must make a show of caring for her. It is only for a short time. Then it will be you and me again, my queen and my love."

I couldn't help myself. I had to ask. "And you will lie with her?"

"You know the answer to that." After a minute of silence, he added, "Tomorrow there will be a formal dinner to welcome the ambassadors. Then I will travel north with Tadukhipa for a few weeks."

I stepped back. "You are leaving me for a few weeks? What am I supposed to do while you are gone?"

"It is my desire that the people see you as an extension of me. You will learn to rule, Nefertiti. You need to see the people, and they need to see you. I will instruct my steward on what to do. Follow his advice, and you will be fine."

"I cannot believe you are leaving me," I said in a flat voice, the weight and importance of his request not registering in my understanding yet.

"It is only for a little while. Please, Nefertiti. Now is the time to be queen. Now is the moment that counts. Think of the future."

I stared at him wide-eyed. "What are you asking me to do?"

He reached his hand out and stroked my wet hair, toying with the ends where it was beginning to curl. "Care for the people, Nefertiti. Just as you cared for the treasures of your tribe. Show my people that you are not just my wife but the true and rightful queen of Egypt. Find some reasonable causes to defend without angering the Amun priests. I trust you in this. I know you will not fail."

I raised my chin in acknowledgment, but I could not hide the hurt in my eyes. I refused to say anything else. What else could I say? I would never change his mind.

With a sigh, he said, "It will be this way whether you like it or not." With those words, my husband left me alone in his chambers, and I had no idea where he went.

I did not wait for him to return. I wiped the tears from my face and returned to my own rooms. The stares I received from some of the servants told me that our argument had not gone unnoticed. Everyone in the palace would know by now. What did I care? Tadukhipa could have her little victory over me. I had Pharaoh's child in my belly! Menmet shuffled behind me and scampered in front of me to open the door.

"Do not worry, Queen Nefertiti. Menmet will help you." She closed the curtains behind us and took my hand, leading me deeper into my chamber. In a whisper, she said, "Tadukhipa will not win."

"Were you listening to our conversation, Menmet?" I frowned at her suspiciously.

"It is no secret, my Queen. This was inevitable. Now is the time to fight and win! You must be our Great Queen. Our Pharaoh needs a good queen to care for his people. I see that you care. Menmet sees. I will help you. Do not cry, beautiful lady." She reached out her open arms, and I fell into them. I cried on her tiny shoulder as she crooned and stroked my hair. When my heart had wrung out all its tears, I sat on a nearby couch and stared out the window. She offered me a cup, but I refused it. I could not dwell on this any longer. I had to think about something else. I wiped at my nose with a handkerchief. It had tiny blue flowers embroidered around the edges. I wondered where I got these from. Some gift from a courtier, I supposed.

"Tell me about your home, Menmet. Where are you from? Have you always served here in Thebes? I can tell by your language that like me, you were not born here."

"No indeed, my Queen, I am not from here. I have been here only for one year, but my older sisters have been here for many years. My father is an Egyptian, yes, but my mother comes from a land in the

East. Priests of Amun cannot marry, did you know?" I turned to look at her and shook my head. "But apparently they can make children." She laughed, but it was not a happy sound. "Well, the highest priests cannot. Still, Heby comes many times to see my mother, and he brings her gifts. He has many daughters but no sons, and he is kind enough to place his many daughters in the courts of Pharaoh."

"Are you the youngest, Menmet?"

"Yes, except one. I have one more sister, Salama, but she is lame and will not walk, no matter how much we plead with the gods on her behalf. Although she is lame, she is clever and can sew beautiful things, like those."

I smiled at her. "She made these for me?"

"Yes." She looked down, embarrassed. "I could not refuse her."

"I love them. The flowers are perfect, and there are no crooked stitches. She is very talented."

"I will tell her. You will make her smile for the rest of her life."

Spontaneously I patted her hand and smiled at her. "Your mother must bring your sister here so that I may meet them both."

Menmet shook her head, her bobbed wig swinging gently as she looked down again. "Oh, no, that can never be. I could not offend you in that way."

"In what way, Menmet? I would never be offended by meeting your sister or your mother."

"Yes, but Salama is not perfect. As I said, she is lame. I cannot bring such imperfection into the presence of the Great Wife of Pharaoh."

"I am not that, and even if I were, I would not enforce such foolish rules. I cannot speak for those who came before me, but I assure you, Menmet, I do not feel that way. All children are treasures and should be treated as such. Where I am from..." I knew I should not speak of the past. I had been reminded on more than one occasion to speak only of the present, to speak only of Egypt not of my Meshwesh upbringing. But I felt I had to correct Menmet. "Where I am from, children are our treasures. All children, even the imperfect ones, are loved and cared for. I do not think otherwise, and neither shall those in my court."

Menmet's round face brightened, and she said, "Thank you for saying so, my Queen. If everyone thought like you, maybe there would be no more sadness and no child offerings. I suppose we are lucky that Salama has not been offered to the fires. Now, let Menmet help you. We must find the best gowns, the best wigs, and the most glorious jewels in all of Egypt. We will show these Hittite savages how we dress in Egypt. They will see who is truly the Greatest Queen!"

"Child offerings? What are you talking about?"

She froze on the spot and answered me as if I were stupid. "The sacrifices. Where the children go, the ones who are imperfect or unwanted for some reason."

I felt sick at the idea. I insisted that she tell me everything she knew. "I want to know about these child offerings. Tell me, Menmet."

"Very well, my Queen." The girl sat down on the painted floor at my feet and sighed. "Sometimes, when a child is born not perfect, maybe she is missing some toes, or her legs are crooked, she is given to the gods. They will receive her, reshape her, and send her again. Most of these memfre children, for that is what the priests call them, go to the temples of Amun. Not all temples accept children, but many do. The priests give the parents money for the children, and then cast the children into the fire. I think Heby wanted to offer my sister to his god. He did not win the argument."

"Fires? What?" I rose to my feet, my hands flying to my stomach again. I felt nausea rising. How could this happen in my husband's kingdom? "Does Amenhotep—I mean, Pharaoh—know about this?"

"I am sure he knows. Everyone does. It is no secret, my Queen, although it is not spoken of...much."

"This is astonishing. How do they justify such cruelties? Who would do such a thing to a child?"

She shook her head and stared down at her hands.

"Does your father do this, Menmet? Is that why you fear him so? Does he threaten you with your sister?"

She nodded without looking up. "She is still young, and my mother grows too feeble to care for her properly. I do not think she will change her mind, but what if she does? What if she were to die?"

"You have no reason to fear, Menmet. Not anymore!" I sprang from my couch and walked to my cedar closets.

"What do you intend to do?" She scrambled to help me. Her voice sounded fearful and uncertain.

"I am not sure yet, but I can tell you what I *don't* intend to do. I do not intend to sit around and do nothing. We must be careful, Menmet, but I will put a stop to this. My husband told me to find a just cause. I have." I snatched a few robes from the closet and tossed them on my bed. Like my husband did when he planned something, I began to pace my chambers. "Tell a messenger to send for my uncle. I will receive him this evening. Also, have my chef arrange a meal for us. We will eat together in the outer chamber."

She started to leave, but I called after her. "And send a scribe, Menmet. I have letters to write. Better make that a scribe who knows the language of Grecia. I want to speak to them in their native tongue."

She bowed quickly and said, "It will be done."

I sighed as I sifted through the colorful robes and gowns. So Tadukhipa had won this round. She used her connections to best me, but it would be an empty victory. I had Amenhotep's heart. If only we had stayed in the Crescent Pool. If only I could dive deep into the waters and swim away from all this. But I couldn't. I had someone else to think about now besides myself. I had a child in my belly and children dying right here in Thebes. In just a few minutes, my mind had shifted completely. I had a purpose now, something to think about other than myself and my husband's petty wife, Tadukhipa.

I might have won Pharaoh's heart, but now I had to win the hearts of his people. I would begin by dealing with this injustice. I prayed for wisdom as I began to think about how I would challenge this foul tradition and bring down these evil priests. Now I had a reason to destroy them. I rejected all the robes I had selected and walked back to the closet. I found a forgotten robe in the back. It had been a gift from Omel, one that I had never expected to wear, but tonight I would. With renewed appreciation, I examined the back. A falcon soared across it, and tiny jewels dropped from its feathers.

If it is my destiny to be the falcon, then I might as well wear the garment.

Chapter Six

A*fter Life—Tiye*

The clumsy servant wrapped my head with the cloth, thinking that I would not see through the flimsy blindfold. What a foolish man! The idea of keeping my husband's grave hidden, even from his wife...as if I would corrupt the body of the only man I had ever loved. These priests took too much upon themselves. What a fool! I did not protest, however, and took the idiot's offered hand while I disembarked from the litter. If he had any intelligence at all, he might have asked himself how I could see his hand. But he did not appear to notice. He led me into the narrow passageway and removed my bandage with a flourish as if I would gasp and swoon over the priests' handiwork. If he thought I would do so, he was doubly a fool.

"Leave me now," I said as I blinked my eyes to adjust them to the light. It was very dim, but there were torches along the walls and I could see the farthest wall in the distance. It was painted with my husband's name and an image of the two of us together holding a lotus flower. I had seen this before. A dozen or so years ago, the builder brought us the model to look at before work ever began. From what I could tell, he had done an excellent job of copying the images and had not missed the details.

The servant left me without protest, and I strolled along the cool tunnel that would lead me to my husband's final resting place. All things had been accomplished. His body would be interred, and soon the tomb would be sealed for all eternity, never to be opened again even for Amenhotep's queen.

They might as well bury my heart here too!

One day, I would rest just on the other side of the thick stone wall that would separate us. The priests said that we would be reunited in death, and until the passing of my husband, I had believed this. But now I was not so sure. Who truly knew the journey of the soul? No one could explain it to me, not to my satisfaction, and I had searched for assurances for months. In our many years together, Amenhotep and I had whispered promises to one another concerning our deaths. He would come to me, and I would come to him.

I walked alongside the painted walls and examined the paintings. As I drew closer, I could plainly see Amenhotep's broad shoulders and strong arms. The massive painting became even more breathtaking as I entered the room. "My love," I whispered. I stood before the cold stone wall and touched it lovingly with my fingers. I traced the cartouche, reading it a hundred times. I cared not if anyone saw me. I laid my head against the wall and whispered his name, but he did not answer.

Oh, how I wished I had taken the knife and cut my own throat when I heard the news! Oh, how I wished I had thrown myself off the top of my palace! But here I stood, coward that I was, alive, even though many days I felt dead and empty.

I leaned against the wall with the cartouche at my back and took in the view of the room. It had a low ceiling, but there was no shortage of furniture fit for a king. The firelight sparkled off the tips of the golden spears. Here was Amenhotep's chariot and everything he would need to go to war in the Otherworld. It was surreal to think of him at war with someone in the Land of the Dead. Would he see Thutmose, our dear son? I sighed into the silence. No answers came. I traveled about the room, touching all my husband's things one last time. As I did, my mind wandered.

Once, when I was young, I drank from the Navel of Isis. The strange pink concoction had overcome me for many days after I consumed it. Unlike some priestesses, I never took another drink of that ghastly brew again. I did not enjoy the experience, the feeling that I had no control, the blurriness of my memories. And I wanted to remember. Indeed, the older I got, the more difficult it was to remember recent events. But the past—oh, it was so near. I felt again as if I were drunk from the sacred drink, but somehow I had fallen into the depths of sorrow unable to recover. How long had it been since I'd seen my son?

I found another portrait of Amenhotep. I kissed the wall and rubbed my hands along it again as I explored a nearby corridor. These rooms were also filled with Amenhotep's things. Some new, some old. I could see his collection of jewelry, all pieces polished and shining in open boxes, just waiting for the Pharaoh to claim them again.

I kept walking.

In the next room, there were sealed jars of wine, baskets of bread and garlic, and all sorts of foods, all made of stone. It must last for all eternity. What better ingredient than stone? I walked down the corridor and found another room full of the discarded items from Amenhotep's life. These were more personal, more revealing of the man Amenhotep truly was. There were rows of sandals, piles of folded laundry including linen gowns, sumptuous silk robes, and many crowns. I opened the nearby chest and saw that it was full of armbands, all in different colors. I picked them up and then let them fall back to the chest. I closed the chest and stood in the hallway. There were many more rooms to explore, but I did not need to look any further. I could see that all things had been given the appropriate attention and that all things had been done for Pharaoh, just as he commanded. The only thing that was not here was his body. It would be delivered tonight. His priests alone would attend the actual burial.

I walked out of his tomb, feeling as if I had left my own soul behind. The bumbling servant greeted me, asking if all was well. I mumbled my approval to him and was lifted into the litter. I didn't struggle when he covered my eyes again. A few minutes later, we made another stop, this time at my own tomb. Finally, my resting place was ready to receive my body. I found the timing ironic. Perhaps it was wishful thinking on their part that after all this time my grave was ready. I could almost hear their thoughts: *As soon as the old king's tomb was readied, he died—maybe this is a portent! The old queen will die too!*

The truth was, I had insisted that this be done immediately, believing the whole time that soon I would join Amenhotep. But each day the sun rose, and I was still alive.

Without waiting for the stupid attendant to remove the bandage, I snatched it from my head, ignoring his look of disapproval. *Kill me, then, brave one!* I thought, scowling back at him.

I walked with my head held high into my newly finished tomb. The walls were gaily colored with bright blue peacocks, a palm-lined river flowed along the expanse of it, and a collection of birds fluttered above it all. If by chance I was not permitted into the Otherworld and had to dwell here for eternity, I would at least have something pleasant to look at. Along the entrance wall were portraits of my family. I smiled at seeing the image of my brown-skinned Thutmose and my own parents. How small they appeared to me now! I could also see the list of the names that my beloved had given me over the years. I did not take the time to read them, for I knew them all by heart.

Hereditary Princess, Lady of the Two Lands, Great King's Wife, Mistress of Upper and Lower Egypt, Keeper of Pharaoh's Heart.

What did any of these titles mean now? What wouldn't I have given to spend one more day sailing across the lake with my husband by my side? What wouldn't I have given to lay my head in his lap and feel his hands stroke my hair? I walked to the back of the tomb and into the inner chamber that would hold my sarcophagus. I lay on the golden bier and stared at the ceiling. It had been lovingly painted with stars and heavenly sights. I closed my eyes and crossed my arms over my chest, pretending to be dead. What if I could die? I was strong. I could just will myself to die, couldn't I?

Oh, Amenhotep! Let me come to you now! Summon me, my love!

My words echoed through the chamber, trembling in the air. I waited, hoping to hear my husband's voice ring through the emptiness, but alas, I heard nothing. Only the beating of my heart, the pulsing of my blood, my shallow breathing. Determined, I remained still, my arms across my chest in the figure of one who was dead. These actions availed me nothing. I lived still. I sighed into the darkness and whispered once again, "Amenhotep, call me to you. Call me to you, and I will run like a gazelle. Call me to you, and I will crush my own heart to obey. Call me to you, and I will seal myself into these rooms and wait for death to take me. Tell Osiris that I long to join you, I, your rightful wife and Queen of Egypt."

I heard nothing for a long while and then the rustling of something. Quiet at first, then louder, clearer. It was something dry, something unseen. "Amenhotep, is that you?" I whispered, my faithless heart pounding like a tightly bound drum. I heard the sound again and did not move.

Then I heard his voice. Not in the air and not in my ears, but I heard it in my heart. His words came to me: *Remember our sons. The one alive, the one who is dead. Remember your promise to me. Do what I failed to do.* With a gasp, I sat up, swinging my short legs over the side of the cold metal stand. I slid off the box and scanned the room, hoping to see the tall figure of my husband. For a second, I did see a shadow looming in the corner. Then it faded. It was nothing. I knew it was a foolish thing to hope for. He was dead; I had seen him dead. I had visited the embalmers. I knew Amenhotep was gone. Whether by his own choice or by the gods, he was gone. But my promise to him lived on, and I must obey it. I must keep it. For him and for my sons.

"Yes, husband. I remember my promise to you. I will do as you ask, and then I will join you, my love. Prepare a place for me!"

I heard nothing but the soft rustling again and walked out of my tomb with a new resolve. As much as I longed for death, even embraced it, my work here was not yet done. I had heard his voice, and that was proof to me that he was not yet at rest. I would not fail him. I stepped out of the dark tomb, rubbing my hands along the cool wall. I did not hesitate in the doorway but stepped into the sun, embracing its warmth by turning my face to it. I breathed in the dusty air and climbed into my litter, waving away the servant who would attempt to blindfold me once again.

"Don't be a fool! This is my tomb. Do you think that I would rob myself? Do you think that I would tell someone where I shall lie? Move out of my way." Surprised at my abruptness, the man stepped back with his gold cloth in his hand. Memre, my faithful servant, waited in the litter for me. I said to her, "We must go see the new Queen. There are things that I must do—that we must do." With a grim nod, Memre gave the order, and the litter began to move. We had barely exited the valley before she and I had worked up our plan. Nefertiti must be queen, and I must have my revenge.

The Desert Queen had not been the quick study I had hoped for, but in truth, I had abandoned her to wallow selfishly in my grief. The time for that was ended. I was sure the Monkey had not spent her time mourning my husband.

"Have they arrived yet?" She did not ask me who. Besides Huya, Memre knew my thoughts better than anyone. It was the Hittites I spoke of, the grasping, deceitful Hittites.

"Yes, and their mission is clear. Even now, your son is entertaining them, listening to them, hoping to follow in his father's footsteps and keep peace between the kingdoms. What lies is the Hittite woman pouring into his ear?"

"He will entertain her for a time because he is Pharaoh, but it would take much more than some sweet words to lure him away from Nefertiti. Of that, I am sure. The boy is smitten with her—I had to do little more than introduce the two of them. Nothing less than Fate brought them together."

She snorted. "Are you Fate now, my Queen? Is that one of the titles of Isis? If I remember correctly, the same could be said for you and your husband, but you still had to fight to keep him."

"Do not mock me!" I barked at her. As usual, she shrugged it off, and I continued, "What can these Hittites offer my son besides a spoiled princess? What would lure him away from his Desert Queen? What threat is there?"

"Perhaps there is none. Like you say, these are merely formalities."

I tapped my lip with my finger and looked at her through slitted eyes. "What are you not telling me?"

"Would I keep anything from you, my Queen? In regard to Tadukhipa, I know nothing beyond what you already know. However, when I visited Nefertiti, I saw she had the daughter of Heby in her retinue."

"Heby's daughter? When did this happen? Why was I not consulted?"

"You would not allow me in your room, my Queen. I do not know who made the arrangements for Nefertiti's court, but I can tell you that there are a great many questionable characters in her circle."

I straightened and gave her a wrinkled frown. "Well, we shall see about that. I'm anxious to meet Heby's daughter and see what other snakes are slithering in the grass."

We rode the rest of the way in silence except for the flickering of my fan and the footsteps of my attendants. I could hear the boisterous sounds of the city as we approached. Thebes was not a quiet place—and it had taken on quite a frenzied feeling of late. With so many new visitors to court, if you could count the Hittites as new, and the arrival of the surprisingly exciting Desert Queen, there was much to be done. Courtiers from around Egypt had arrived hoping to catch a glimpse of the beautiful young monarch and her handsome Pharaoh. Of course, there were also other factions present, including those representing Kiya and other families, great families, noble families who hoped

Pharaoh would look with kindness upon their households and bring their daughters into such elevated states of grace. It was the dream of all noble families to marry into Amenhotep's bloodline. And since there was no limit to the number of wives an Egyptian king could have, all things were possible. Even now Amenhotep's neglected harem was ridiculously large. I would never wish my daughter to fill a spot in the harem, as it was a lonely life, but many fathers did just that.

"What of Sitamen? How does she fare in her new palace? She has not been to see me since her father passed to the Otherworld."

"Perhaps we should go see her first, my Queen. A visit from her mother would do her good."

It was my turn to snort in derision. I remembered that Memre had a particular softness for my daughters, especially Sitamen. Detecting my attitude, she wisely said nothing else. How could I explain to her the complexity of my feelings for my daughter? Finally, the swaying slowed. I could tell the attendants were tired, for their feet shuffled clumsily after walking for hours in the heat. I happily shuffled out of the litter, resisting the urge to rub my tired back and behind. How queenly would that have been? Instead, I walked straight up the steps to one of the cool patios. This was my son's palace, and I would not rush into his courts during his negotiations, no matter how much I hated Tadukhipa's people. He had enough to think about now. I quietly vowed to visit him in a day or two before I returned home. It had been too long since I had seen his handsome face, a face so much like his father's.

Immediately a flurry of activity surrounded me. I took a seat and allowed the various attendants to meet my needs. I whispered to Memre, and she left me to do my bidding. I did not have to wait long.

"Great Queen," the young Queen called to me. She bowed, and to my surprise greeted me with the sacred Isis gesture. With a delighted smile, I returned the gesture and invited her to sit with me.

"Queen Nefertiti, how well you look. I trust my son is treating you well."

She could not hold back her smile. "He is the best of husbands, my Queen. Does he know you are here? I am sure he would want to see you." I took her hand and squeezed it. Yes, she was a beautiful girl, but still too kind, too trusting. I could see that in her eyes. *We will have to drive that out of her.* I also saw something else. What was that? Fear? Loneliness? Ah, she would have to get used to that. Fear and loneliness were a queen's constant companions.

"I will see him soon. It is you I came to see, Queen Nefertiti." I looked at Memre, and without saying a word, she collected the servants and shooed them away so that my daughter-in-law and I could speak alone. She appeared to breathe a sigh of relief. "How are things between you two? Memre tells me you are with child. Is it true?"

"Yes, it is true."

"Then why are there no banners? No celebration? Egypt should know that a new Prince or Princess is soon to arrive. Surely your steward has instructed you in these things. The arrival of a child into your household is a holy, wonderful event, and it must be respected. Who do you have advising you?"

"I did as you asked me to. I made peace with my uncle. We have visited, and I have given him some tasks, but I have not planned on doing anything special yet in regard to the announcement of my child—our child. As you know, Amenhotep is in the middle of negotiating with the Hittites over their daughter and other things. I did not wish to complicate matters."

"Nonsense! Your child is the child of Pharaoh. I can promise you that Tadukhipa would offer you no such relief. She would insist on every advantage being bestowed upon her. You must do nothing less. It is a good thing that I have come, for your advisers, whoever they may be, are seriously derelict in their duties."

Nefertiti appeared troubled, and I immediately felt sympathy for her. It was hard being a new queen—especially an outsider, someone with no allies or influential friends. I had been away for too long. Why had Amenhotep not spoken to her about these things? Perhaps I had neglected them both. I chewed on the inside of my lip and peered at her, then said, "No matter. I'm here now, and I will help you. I can see you have something on your mind. What is it?"

"Amenhotep is leaving. He is taking a trip with Tadukhipa. He says it is to please the Hittites only, that his heart is not hers, but I know how things are. For all his strength, he is but a man, and Tadukhipa, a very cunning woman."

"There is nothing you can tell me about Tadukhipa that would surprise me. She was my sister-wife long before she was yours, but I know my son. She can throw whatever she likes at him. Flirtatious looks, succulent dishes, extravagant gifts, even decadent pleasures. Amenhotep is a man of character. A thinking man and not one to be won with a few back rubs or guilty pleasures. You are thinking like a commoner. And Tadukhipa is no common street whore. She is royalty, even if it is barbarian royalty. She was raised at a large court, which gives her an advantage over you, but I have no doubt that my son loves you and will put you above all his other wives, including his sister."

"He says that he cannot think only of himself but of all Egypt. He has made no promises to me, and I am to be left here to sit upon his throne. I'm glad you are here, for I do not know what to do." Suddenly she grasped my hands. "Promise me you will stay with me, Great Queen."

I had to remind myself not to flinch or slap her. I was not used to being handled. I took a deep breath and said, "If he has asked you to sit on his throne, he has afforded you a great privilege. He has never asked Tadukhipa to do such a thing. He is giving you the opportunity to show the people of Egypt that you are indeed truly worthy of the title of Great Wife. Do not disappoint him. I will spend a few days with you, but beyond that, these things are up to you. I have my own destiny to fulfill, Nefertiti."

Then she asked me a surprising question. "Why did you pick me, Queen Tiye? Of all the women in the Red Lands and the Black Lands, why did you pick me? For I know it was you who orchestrated all this."

I looked deeply into her green eyes. She deserved an answer, but the truth was I did not know what led me to compel her to stay with me. Perhaps it was the desert blood that ran in our veins, calling us to one another. Perhaps it was the sight of her glorious red hair trailing down her narrow back—a true sign of the gods. Perhaps it was her willingness to give everything for her tribe. If she had refused my conditions, would I have helped her?

"I compelled you to stay because you were always meant to be here. This is your place. Not because I said so, and not because my son loves you, but because you were meant to be here. This is your destiny, Nefertiti." She nodded, acknowledging my words, and I added, "I have found it is better to spend less time questioning why and more time thinking about serving your Pharaoh. It helps to keep things in perspective. There is nothing outside of him. No god or goddess. Not even your children can you love as much as you love him." Suddenly my stomach rumbled, and hunger struck me as if it were a tangible thing.

The young queen must have heard my stomach's complaints, for she quickly said, "It would be my honor if you would join me for the evening meal. We can dine in my room where it is cool and quiet. I value your opinion, Great Wife."

I was sure that my presence was known all over the palace by now, so it would do us little good to hide out in the queen's chambers. However, this would serve as the perfect opportunity to meet her servants in an informal atmosphere. I agreed, and together we strolled to her rooms. We walked in silence, and as I passed by the familiar painted columns and marble statues, I remembered happier days. The echo of Thutmose's laughter. The playful giggles of my daughters.

Amenhotep's booming voice as he called his many dogs to his side. To Egypt the palace was a grand place, a thing of beauty, a copy of the mansion of heaven. But to me it had been home. It felt good to be home again.

Chapter Seven

*C*hoices—*Sitamen*

I rubbed the sandalwood oil all over my hands and arms as I enjoyed the peaceful quiet of my solitary bathhouse. I stared down into the palms of my small hands. I could hardly believe the things they had done just a few days ago. The blood—oh, so much blood—and the squirming, wriggling life they had held.

I would never forget how the smell of the blood filled my nostrils, how it offended me. Warriors like Ramose must have smelled it all the time since they hacked, murdered, and maimed as part of their careers. The general waited for me now, and my anticipation of the meeting surprised me. Rubbing the oil furiously into my cuticles, I thought about the few times we had exchanged words. If I were not Pharaoh's daughter, I was sure he would not know my name.

For someone with so much courage—at least, that was the talk—Ramose knew very little about women. Like most men, he took them at face and figure value. To men like him, women were merely convenient receptacles for their seed, not equal at all. But that was his mistake.

I stared into the mirror and made an honest assessment of the face that stared back at me. Small like my mother but with longer arms and legs, I had an angular face like my father. I also had his full lips and clear, smooth olive skin. Unlike the rest of the court, I had grown my hair back over the past few years, and it was a decision I did not regret. Doing so gave me a power and confidence I had not expected. I brushed my hair and let the dark brown cascades fall around my face. I no longer wore a crown except during those rare matters of state when anyone remembered to summon or include me. I preferred to leave my head bare, but as that was not acceptable for royalty, I did as the Persian women did, wearing jewels on my forehead and a wide necklace about my neck. These were my only adornments today. My brows were naturally heavy, but I'd recently had my servant shape them with wax and was pleased with the results.

My ears were too large, but there was nothing I could do about that except keep them hidden. Tadukhipa often said that my mother frowned when she saw me because I reminded her of the small brown bats she so feared, so large were my ears. I sniffed at the thought.

I had large brown eyes that were expressive, too expressive at times, but I had spent the past few months learning to wear the same mask that my mother wore so well. I'd become a master at controlling my emotions—I had been a child too long. Today would be my first audience with someone outside of my immediate circle of friends, and it would be a test of my abilities.

When my brother gave me this palace, I felt such dismay because I knew that he had sealed my fate. He would not take me as a true wife, as some brothers did their sisters. I would not be so honored and would remain a forgotten minor queen until the day I died. I would never love or be loved by a man. I would never have children. The realization was more than I could bear. I would never forget Tadukhipa's expression of pity as I told her the news. How quickly she forgot me when I was no longer of use to her.

It did not take long to reconsider my thoughts about leaving the Royal Harem. I was glad to be free from the constant pulling and pushing between my mother and Tadukhipa. I was glad to be away from the turmoil caused by the redheaded Desert Queen. What a fool I had been to think that Inhapi and Tadukhipa were my friends! I tossed the brush down in anger, thinking of the latter. Was I not Pharaoh's daughter? Didn't Amenhotep's blood run in my veins? Let them think me a "mouse" as they sometimes called me. Even a mouse had power. I practiced my smile in the mirror while I doused my skin with perfume.

This perfume had been Inhapi's favorite. Whether he wanted to or not, Ramose would find the scent seductive—at least I hoped he would.

"My lady, the general is here."

"Good," I said as I continued to rub my skin until it shone. I had lovely skin, and I intended to show it off. The servant lingered in the doorway as if to hear further instructions from me. I waved my hand dismissively and said, "You may go now. Make the general comfortable, and make sure he has plenty to drink. The good wine, Mariway."

"Yes, lady." The girl scurried away to do my bidding.

I searched my closet for the garment I had in mind. I would wear nothing too grand today. I wanted General Ramose to see me as a woman, not a princess or a cast-off queen. I had to be patient and careful. Men like Ramose did not like to be forced into things. I would have to lead him into my plan.

Not for the first time, I thought about Ramose and the Meshwesh woman. What he ever saw in her, I did not know. I did not understand the attraction. She was neither pretty nor intelligent, but apparently, she had been skilled enough to produce Ramose a son.

I chose a plain tan-colored gown of ethereal fabric. It would float when I walked. The garment had no sleeves and a low neckline that plunged to my navel. I stepped into it and adjusted the straps as I studied myself in the mirror. Yes, this would do quite nicely. Even I could see how much I had changed!

Although I was dressed and ready to meet my guest, I was in no hurry. I wanted to remind Ramose of his rank and standing. Whether he considered me so or not, I was a queen.

I tore pieces from this morning's bread and tossed it to my birds. I loved my birds. I ran my fingers across the bars of the new cages. They were made of gold and were embellished with sapphires. My father and I shared a love for the blue stones. I had many gifts from him. Why should they not adorn the cages of my children? The dozen or so birds chirped with delight as I tossed the pieces into the cages. I poked my hand inside, and one of my favorites hopped onto my finger. As always, I handled them with loving care. My mother had been right. I cared more for these birds than I did for the people around me. Birds were simple, gentle, and loving creatures. They were happy to eat whatever came from my hand, and they provided me with endless songs without requiring coins or some benefit for themselves. I loved them, and when one died I always mourned. I prayed that one day I might become one, in either this life or the next. This was probably a fool's dream—a child's dream—but it was mine.

Nobody could steal dreams, could they?

After I finished chattering with my pets, I returned the tiny brown finch to his home. I dusted the crumbs from my hands and strolled along the columned porch outside my chambers. The sun had been up for quite some time, and the purple irises had fully opened to welcome the sunlight. I poked my nose into one and enjoyed the sweet aroma. The supple petals would not last very long in this heat, but luckily this kind produced blooms often. It never lacked flowers.

This bed of irises had been a thoughtful touch from my brother, who knew how much I loved living things. It was hard to hate him, and indeed I did not. I loved him. He and I had both been lost in the shadow of our dead brother Thutmose, forever hidden from our mother's heart. For a time, we had one another. We were as close as the twin stars, forever together, or so I had believed. I remembered the kind boy he had been. How he used to love bringing me birds and kittens. He never shamed me or mocked me. But that was so long ago, before my mother twisted his mind against me. Before she stole his affection from me! Then she convinced my father to make me his wife and by doing so moved me from our home to the Royal Harem. My father had never claimed his rights as a husband, thankfully, but I had no doubt that my mother had wanted him to do so. "It will be the only way you have children, Sitamen. It is an honor to carry the seed of Amenhotep and your duty to keep our dynasty alive." The idea revolted me, and

I suspected it also offended my father for he never engaged in such behavior. Queen Tiye had tidily removed me from my brother's and father's lives. Like most women she was a deceiver, a betrayer.

I heard shouts coming from below me and peered over the edge of the balcony. I heard Ramose's voice demanding to see me. I smiled to myself. Yes, I knew what I was doing.

A few minutes later, I heard the sound of Mariway's heavy feet padding into my room. "Lady, your guests are waiting in the portico. They've refused food and drink. And..."

"And?" I said, walking toward her calmly, my face a trained mask of control.

"The general demands to see you now. He says it is urgent and that he cannot wait any longer."

I could not help but laugh. To think such a Mouse as I could have such power over a man like Ramose. I was enjoying this more than I had imagined I would.

"Tell the general that I will come when it pleases me. Offer him food and drink again, and make him and his friend comfortable."

The girl looked unhappy to hear those words, but that was not my concern. Fortunately for her, she did not express her unhappiness to me. She padded away again, and I stood on the balcony, hoping to hear the conversation. At that moment my birds decided to break into loud and boisterous songs. It was probably for the best. I waited for another half an hour and then slowly descended the stairs to greet my guests.

Kafta saw me first. He tapped Ramose on the arm to draw his attention. The general had a dark, disapproving scowl on his face, but only for a moment. I could see my improvements had not escaped his notice. That pleased me and warmed my skin. I reminded myself not to look away or appear to notice. I stood at a distance. I welcomed them to my palace and gestured for them to follow me. It was another moment, another opportunity to demonstrate my power to the general. I was in charge here. This was not my brother's palace or the Royal Harem. I traveled the long hallway with the general and his man behind me. I did not engage them in conversation or turn my attention away from my destination. As I had instructed, my servants had gathered in the hallway and bowed obediently as we passed by them. I led my guests out of the palace, down the steps and to the grotto. Until I came to this place, I had never seen such a grotto. I lived in an exquisite prison full of hidden delights.

Before we entered the tunnel that would lead us to the child, I paused. "Please wait here," I said to Kafta even as I waved Ramose ahead. Kafta shot Ramose a raised eyebrow, and the general nodded.

"As you wish," the bowlegged warrior grumbled before leaving us to walk through the grotto alone. At this point, I did not make him walk behind me. I could tell my change in position made him uncomfortable, but he did not question it.

"I am sorry about your wife, General Ramose. I know she was a great favorite at court."

"Yes, she will be missed. Forgive me, Princess, if I do not feel talkative. I had given up hope on seeing my son, but to hear that he's here with you...I have to admit I am curious to know how he ended up in your care. And..."

We stepped out of the shady grotto and into the sunlit courtyard. Young servants milled about performing their tasks for the child. I had not left out a thing, and I wanted Ramose to see what good care his child had been in. There were small animals, a child's pool, and many other amenities to enjoy. "I will answer all your questions, but first..." I waved Naomi toward me. In her arms was the precious, active bundle, the son of Ramose. I pushed my hair behind my shoulder and accepted the squirming child. He was quite handsome, despite being only a few days old. I gave Ramose a small smile and said, "General, meet your son."

I held the bundle up slightly and watched the man's face soften. I had known the soldier all my life, and like many ladies in the court, I had admired his handsome face. I was pleased to see him immediately reach for the baby. Many men, including my own father, did not care to handle their offspring. I could see Ramose was not that kind of man, and that made me want him even more.

Yes! He is the one for me!

Funny that I should want him at all. He had been unfaithful to Inhapi. She knew all about his dalliances but did not seem to mind. I would have been wroth with jealousy had he been my husband. The past few weeks, I had tended to his latest lover, at least until the child was born.

I hadn't been sure what I would do about Ramose until just now. I would never have children, not in the way most women had them. I would have to adopt mine, and what better child to adopt than the noble child of a decorated general? It was not an easy thing to want, but I wanted this baby, and I wanted Ramose!

"Like this," I said with a soft laugh as he fumbled with his grip on the child. I led him by the arm to the shade and invited him to sit as he held his son. The soft white cloth of the child's blanket appeared even whiter next to the general's sun-bronzed skin. For the first time I could remember, Ramose smiled a smile from the heart. It was a big smile that spread across his face, making him even more handsome, and I saw the fringes of his lashes wet with unexpected tears. My heart leapt at the sight of it. Oh, yes, things were going nicely.

"He is well? Not sick or weak?"

"He is the strongest child I have ever seen. You should be proud of him. He will grow to be a strong warrior."

His deep voice rumbled, "I am proud of him." He finally looked me fully in the eyes, and I caught my breath. "Thank you, Princess."

"The pleasure is mine," I said, touching the child's soft hair with my finger.

"Is he always so quiet?"

I laughed. "No, indeed, he is not. He can cry quite loudly when he is hungry, but we do not let him cry long. I have a wet nurse here who loves to dandle him at her breast."

He smiled at that and stared again into the sleeping child's face. "I do not want him spoiled. He is a soldier's son and will be a soldier himself one day." I nodded and sat in silence, watching him count toes and fingers. "I wish he would open his eyes so I might see them."

"He has two," I said playfully. "Look in any mirror, General, and you will see them, for he has the eyes of his father."

"Please, call me Ramose."

I felt my face flush and said, "Very well, Ramose." Just at that moment, the child began to squirm and fuss as if he knew we were speaking of him. Ramose appeared nervous, and I smiled gently. "Let me take him. It is time to feed. See? He is a strong boy." I scooped up the child and handed him to Naomi, who sped away with him to find the baby's nurse.

I returned to my seat, leaning back on the cushion, I swung my feet up beside me. It seemed odd being so casual with a man, especially Ramose, but I wanted to enjoy every second.

"His name is Kames."

"Kames is a good name, and I am sure it will be on the lips of many throughout his life."

My answer pleased him, but he appeared unsure of me. "Forgive me for not telling you that Ayn was with me. I know that by doing so, I extended your grief and worry, but you have to understand, I had only your son's welfare in mind."

"What do you mean? Is she still alive?"

I sipped from the cup of water that sat between us and met his eyes fully. "I was returning from visiting the Green Temple when my servant ran to tell me the news. It was then that I saw Ayn running from the palace and heard the commotion. She had a bruised face and blood on her hands. I hid her in the wine cellars under the Blue Gate for a few days, then moved her out of the city. When my brother gave me this palace as a gift, I brought her here. She was barely able to stand by then, so pregnant was she. I was convinced that she would have the baby immediately, but her pregnancy lasted longer than I expected. She stayed in those rooms there until she..."

He said nothing, so I continued, "I don't know what made me hide her. I just did. I cannot explain my actions, Ramose. I wanted to bring her out many times, but I was afraid for the child. After the horrible thing that happened with Inhapi, Tadukhipa was so angry that I was sure she would kill both the mother and the child. She said that she would, and I knew she did not care about arousing the wrath of my brother, his wife or anyone else. She had fallen out of his favor by that time. And you know how much she cared for Inhapi."

I blushed at my memories of the two women together. I had seen them often but had never participated in their activities. I did not know how much Ramose knew about his wife's practices, so I spoke cautiously. "I spoke with Kafta one afternoon and asked for his help. He advised me on how to move forward. I apologize for holding the truth back from you."

"She is dead?"

I met his gaze with steely resolve. "I wish I could give you better news, but perhaps it is for the best. She has met her fate."

He swallowed but said nothing else for a long time. Small birds sailed into the courtyard and skittered about searching for treats. I had similar birds in my menagerie but none as lovely as these, with bold purple and blue feathers. I chided myself for wanting to capture them and put them in one of my pretty cages—I had plenty of birds. Why did I want the ones I could not possess? I should have had more pity, more appreciation for their freedom. But even more, I wanted to possess Ramose. He needed me, I would show him how much, but I had to move slowly. I had some skill in these matters. I had been observing the women in the harem all my life.

"What can I give you to thank you, Princess?" Ramose always addressed me as "princess," despite the fact that I had been a queen for many years. It used to irritate me, but now I liked hearing him call me by that title. I liked thinking that he still saw me as a princess of Egypt, not a forgotten queen doomed to dwell in this lavish prison except on the rare occasions when I was allowed to venture out. Hearing it made it easier to believe that I had a choice—that I still had a future.

"No thanks are necessary, Ramose. It was a joy to help bring Kames into the world. He is a beautiful child."

"I have taxed your hospitality long enough. I will take my son home now."

"Wait!" I stood swiftly. "Please stay a little while. You asked me what you could give me." Shielding his eyes from the sun that rose above us, he looked into my face. It stung my heart to see the distrust, but I smiled at him pleasantly and said, "Stay with me. At least for today. I do not receive many guests, and I would like to hear news about my brother." I knew he wanted to refuse me. "Please," I added.

I couldn't give him my proposal yet. I needed more time because I knew he would refuse me if I told him now. He needed to trust me, to listen to reason. The dark circles under his eyes and the haggard look he wore told me that Ramose had not been cared for in a while. He needed me, even if he did not yet know it.

"If it pleases you, then I am happy to stay for a little while," he added. "Once again, you show me honor I do not deserve. I find you very much grown, Princess. Very different from the girl who used to hang on her father's neck. Tell me, do you still keep birds?"

"Please, call me Sitamen. It has been a long time since anyone has called me by that name. It is music to my ears and makes me feel young."

He laughed, and it was a pleasant but unpracticed sound. I doubted he had done much laughing lately. "You are very young still. If it pleases you, I will call you Sitamen, at least when we are alone." I suppressed a beaming smile into a demure one. In spite of himself, Ramose was flirting with me. That was something, at least.

"That pleases me greatly. Thank you for the indulgence."

As he stood, he looked tired, even more tired than earlier. "Princess, one more thing, and this may sound strange. I would like to see Ayn. Is her body here?"

I clasped my hands in front of me as casually as I could. "Oh, dear. The woman's body is no longer here. I asked the priestesses from the Green Temple to retrieve her. She should be...she is likely no more now." I had to think quickly. No man could enter the Green Temple, but Ramose was a resourceful man. He would find a way if he could. I added, "I know you cared for her, so I ordered her consigned with all honors."

"Consigned?" he asked. The suggestion appeared repulsive to him, and if I had thought about it, I would have answered him differently. I honestly had not expected him to care. That was an oversight. He was disappointed, but I could not allow him to probe deeper into my lie.

I frowned at him in mock surprise. "Was I wrong to do so? I am afraid I do not know what gods she served. Have I offended you?"

"No, you have not. Thank you for your thoughtfulness."

With a nod of dismissal, I left him in the courtyard. He wasted no time in going to find Kames. I could hear his sandals slapping on the stones as he walked into the child's rooms. Now I had to focus on my task. He had to see that leaving the boy with me was the best option. A child needed a mother.

And Ramose needed me.

Chapter Eight

F*ire and Water—Pah*
        My head itched like a hundred angry ants were biting me. I rubbed it and felt nothing but fuzz. The itching was inside my head, not on my skin. It was a strange sensation. Surprised at feeling something besides smooth skin, I could not stop touching my head. At last, my hair was returning. Unfortunately, along with it came my memory. I wished I could forget.

My memories came at me in a tangled ball, and the unhappy ones always arose together like an unwelcome group of friends. With those memories came the emotions in a dark mass of ugliness—ugliness all of my own making. My captor Magg slept beside me, and I sighed at the sound of her snoring. It was difficult enough falling asleep without the older woman's night sounds ringing in my ears. Sleeping with someone did not bother me. I had spent most of my nights with my sister. She did not snore but often talked in her sleep. I suddenly wished I could reach out to her and touch her hair or skin. How that used to comfort me, and I longed for comfort before I fell asleep again and slipped into another nightmare.

Sometimes in my dreams, the Kiffians came with their pawing hands and biting mouths and...other things to violate me. I would awaken in smothered screams with Magg leaning over me, seemingly immune to the power of my blows. She never struck me back but chided me in her own language, I assumed. Magg's lack of teeth did not help me discern what she was saying. I soon gave up, and so did she. Now we communicated mostly with looks and gestures, but she never failed to wake me from the nightmares. For that, I was grateful.

In the past few weeks, or at least I thought it had been that long, I had seen more faces than Magg's. A bevy of priestesses questioned me daily about my home, where I was from, and what I knew about their goddess. Their endless questions tired me, and I felt no obligation to answer them, not at first.

"We know you can see in the fire and water," they would say to me. "Tell us what you see. Can you see our Pharaoh?" I refused to look in the flames or lean over the pools at first, but my hunger and thirst got the better of me. Sometimes it was easy to go without food, but there were times when my body screamed louder than my mind. They knew. The priestesses knew I could not hold out forever. So, they watched and waited. Daily I demanded that they release me and allow me to go home, but daily they did not. A pot of tea was always by my bedside when I woke for the morning ministrations. One day Magg mumbled at me, trying to compel me to drink. I would not. Believing that I refused because I feared poison, she poured herself a cup, drank it, called me "stupid" (I think), and then walked out. After that, I drank the tea without fear, but sometimes I took only a sip or two. Farrah had taught me that sometimes poisons worked slowly, so slowly that you did not know they were working at all. I sipped and waited for death. It never came.

Instead, something else happened. Magg's occasional attempts at language seemed easier to understand. Other things I did not expect began to manifest. Each morning after a dose of the tea, I would feel more peaceful than ever before, and I had a greater awareness of my own soul. As awareness rose within me, the burning fires of ambition diminished. I had nothing to prove, and for the first time in a long time, I felt fear ebb and release its cruel grip on my heart. During the trials, I would have said I feared nothing, but now I knew that was not true. I feared everything.

Nakmaa, the priestess—the high priestess, as near as I could tell—helped me discern the layers of fear within me. She told me that by doing so, I would be free. Free to live without fear. I quickly identified the fear of being bested by my sister, the fear of losing. I also feared the madness that had claimed my mother and caused her to lie down in the sand and leave me behind.

The drink was such an effective medicine that I began to ask for it, and the priestesses happily gave it to me. Of course, their ministrations came with a price, and they were still tight-lipped about how I came to be in the Green Temple. They either did not know or did not think it necessary for me to know. I suspected it was the former. We were in our own world inside the temple. It was like being in a harem, I supposed, without the hope of seeing the man you loved. Some priestesses did entertain guests, male guests, but the men were carefully kept out of sight. I stopped asking about the guests and how I managed to find my way here. Despite my mind's renewal, I had no recollection of those events, but I figured eventually it would come. I began to feel more confident that I *would* remember.

When the priestesses were satisfied that I knew nothing that would help them politically, they took advantage of my other gifts. "Look! Look in the fire, bright-eyed sister. Tell us what you see." I would drink, stare into the flames, and pass on what I saw. Much of those visions seemed nothing but nonsense, but the priestesses all seemed impressed.

In one vision, I saw a cow standing by a great pool. The animal's udders were so full that the cow tipped over from the weight, and many of the fish from the nearby waters came to drink from the teats. I giggled at the sight of the brightly colored fish pulling on the cow, but the women hung on my every word. After spending many hours in front of the brazier, they would send me away. I could hear them chattering to one another as I walked down the long, empty hallway. Truthfully it was less a hallway and more a courtyard. Located in the center of the temple, it was the most impressive feature of the building and reminded me of the Timia Oasis. The columns rose like massive palm trees high into the sky above, each one decorated with ornate patterns and colorful pictures that I assumed declared the might of the temple's deity, Isis. There was a row of statues said to be her many faces, but I had given up believing in deities. I, who had been the most faithful of my family, had been betrayed by them.

I sighed on my bed and licked my dry lips. My face and arms were still hot from the flames over which I had hovered for hours earlier, and my eyes felt as if someone had poured great measures of sand into them. Though I was tired beyond belief, peaceful sleep felt like an impossibility.

Instead, I quietly rose from the room I shared with Magg and wandered by the Pool of Isis, hoping that nobody would be there. I'd gone to bed earlier than most. That had been an hour ago. Many times the pools were empty, except for a few old women who believed the waters washed away their aches and pains. They would strip off their clothing, uncaring that their bodies were wrinkled and flabby. They would slip carefully into the warm waters and swim about as if they were girls. I longed to swim with them, but that would mean I must speak to them. I chose the quieter route, pretending I did not see them even when they greeted me kindly.

At the end of the largest pool was a narrow sandy walkway that led to a series of smaller pools and finally a well. I rarely saw anyone come this far. The Green Temple was actually a massive complex, the main temple being the most popular building. There were other buildings to which I had not gained entrance. Perhaps I did not want to know what occurred behind those closed doors.

I first found this place on one of my many forays to find a way out of the temple grounds. The walls of the Green Temple were higher than any I had seen, even higher than Zerzura's, and they often cast long shadows on the walkways and courtyards. A pair of guards stood at each of the three gates. They wore red tunics and had plumes of purple feathers on their helmets. I assumed the men were eunuchs, as they did not look my way (or any woman's way as far as I could tell).

As I walked past the first three pools, I nodded to one young acolyte who lingered mournfully by the water. She had unusually big eyes that were constantly red from crying. I had seen her many times before. I felt sympathy for her but did not approach her or befriend her. There was no escaping this place, and it was better for her to realize that now. If you were here, you would stay here for all the days of your life. She stared at me as if entreating me to linger and talk, but I did not. I dared not. I had conquered my fears, hadn't I? She must conquer hers.

Leaving her sad countenance behind, I came to the smallest of the pools. The water was still and cooler than the large pools. It was fed by an underground spring that kept it fresh and sweet. Heavy ferns grew around it, and the buzz of a few mosquitoes played annoying music in my ear. I sat beside the water and scooped it up in my hands, splashing it on my face and neck. After a few minutes, I felt refreshed and let my toes dangle in the water as I leaned back on my hands. The stars were appearing now. I knew them by heart, as I had known them since childhood, but they did not comfort me as they once did.

I suddenly longed for Alexio. He would not know where to find me. "The world is a large place with endless spots for hiding," he told me when we were small. How I wished then to be a boy, able to leave my family behind to see the world! Once I almost convinced him to take me with him, to dress me as a boy and stuff me in his caravan so that I too could see the land of the jinn in Petra. He would laugh indulgently and pretend that he would do so, but he never did.

Over time, I did not wish to be a boy anymore. I was glad I was a girl because Alexio began to notice me in new and exciting ways. He noticed my dark eyelashes and the playful tip of my nose, the curve of my face. He did not tell me, but a woman knows these things, even a young one. I was even gladder when he began to play with my hair, brush his hands against mine, smile at me in the way a man would smile at a woman he loved. He toyed with me—I knew it even as a girl—but how thrilling it had been when he kissed me! For him, it had been meaningless, but for me, it had been everything. I loved him, utterly and completely. Until I knew that to him, I was only a means to an end—a way to get to my sister. And then other feelings began to rise to the surface...

I cast a handful of silky white petals into the pool and watched them slowly sink out of sight. A strange bird and other animals made night noises, but I was not afraid of them. This was not the desert. I knew nothing could harm me here.

Except those that lingered outside, hovering between this world and the next.

So far, the spirits had not crossed the temple threshold. But if I stepped outside, I could only imagine what they would do to me. Who said the dead couldn't harm the living? I saw many things in the fire and in the water. Sometimes Farrah's face passed before mine, her eyes full of hatred, her white hair bloody, and her skin black. Other times it was Paimu's grasping hands and silent scream that demanded justice. Of the two, it was her murder that I most regretted, for it had been done in my madness. My jealousy had killed her as much as my blade had. Farrah's death was different. She had brought my blood to a boil, not because of her accusations, but because she dared accuse me when she herself had done murder. And I knew the truth. She had allowed my mother to die. She did that! I saw it in the fire! She sat back and watched and did not lift a finger to help her. She thought no one would ever know. She was wrong.

Paimu, though...she was another story. She did not deserve what happened to her. The truth was, I was a woman possessed that night. Enraged that Alexio had rejected me once again. Enraged that I must lie with Yuni, for I hated the man. Enraged that my uncle came to me once again, reminding me of our secret. Driving the knife into her was like killing myself, only it wasn't me who died. I buried her when it was over, and for a little while, she remained hidden. Until she came back.

I shivered in the moonlight and sat still. I could hear someone walking toward me. The crunching of fallen flowers sent the shivers running down my spine. Could my thoughts have summoned the girl here? I didn't know whether to stand up or try to hide. I decided to do neither. I might as well face whatever justice was coming for me. What would it matter if someone found me dead by a pool? Nobody cared. Nobody who mattered. Most here thought I was mad anyway.

"Hafa-nu, queen's sister," said the small figure who had paused on the path. As the clouds above shifted, the moonlight fell on us, and I could see her more clearly. It was not Paimu.

The woman before me was small. She wore a simple white gown, but everything else about her declared she was someone of importance, including the twin snake bracelets that wrapped around her arms. They reminded me of my father's. I wondered sometimes if he missed me. My visitor had intelligent dark eyes, and I could see that her heart was heavy. She reminded me of someone, but I could not place her. I stood, but only to show her I was much taller than she. "I am the Great Wife of the Pharaoh Amenhotep, although he is now in the Eternal City."

"How is it you greet me so? Do you know the words you speak, or do you just say them because you have heard others speak them?"

"The desert is in my blood. I was born to the Algat, although I claim no mother but Isis now. I remember the Old Ways and the Old Words."

"I have seen your face in the water. They killed your son, didn't they? Left him lying in the paws of the Sphinx, a bloody tribute to their god. Is it justice you seek?"

My question clearly surprised her, and she stumbled toward me. Her dark eyes grew wide as she moved closer to see my face. "So, it is true. You *do* see!"

I did not feel compelled to prove that I could see anything at all, but it appeared that the priestesses had been talking. I said nothing.

"I could command you to look, for it is in my power to do so. Any priestess here would be glad to serve me, and many do. There are things I need to know, and you have the ability to tell me. Are you willing to help me or not?"

If she wanted me to rebel, to bristle at her importance, I did not give her that satisfaction. Death did not frighten me, only the half-dead. Those who lingered. If she killed me, I would be dead and free from seeing them waiting for me. Perhaps I deserved to die. No, there was no guessing. I did deserve it. I wanted to ask, *Why don't these many priestesses help you, then?* But I did not. "Help you how, Queen Tiye? Whatever you might think, I cannot command what I see. I just see. Seeing the past or the future is not for any of us to command, I think."

With a great sigh of weariness, she waved her hand and said, "I did not mean to offend you. It is just my way. People like wasting my time, and I am not a woman who tolerates fools. But I see you aren't either."

"My name is Pah. I am the sister of Nefret, the one you call Nefertiti. I do see in the fire and the water. And I have seen you before, in the flames. The goddess here shows me your face often. She watches you, I think."

The older woman's face softened. I could see that my answer pleased her, but it did not matter to me one way or the other. Without waiting for an invitation, she sat beside the pool and patted the ground, bidding me do the same. It did not take a seer to know that she cared nothing about me. The queen only wanted to know what I saw about her and her family.

I sat back down, determined to feel unimpressed by my unexpected guest. No one had visited me before. Not even Nefret. I put my feet back in the water, enjoying the sensation of the fish nibbling at my toes. Somewhere behind me, I thought I heard a strange sound, as if someone were scratching on metal. I was not certain if this was real or something else, so I said nothing about it.

"What about the water? Do you ever see my face there?" Her voice sounded whispery and young. Much younger than she was, for I guessed she was as old as Farrah was when she died. I wondered if the queen knew I had killed the Old One. But how could she?

"Only in the flames. I see you only in the flames." I let the weight of my words fall on her. If she knew anything about such things, she would know what that meant. If she did not, who was I to burden her with such knowledge?

"Are you happy here?"

I kept my eyes averted and my voice even. Over the years, I had taught myself to hide my true feelings, and this talent came in handy now, for I did not trust the tiny queen. How could I believe the Great Queen of Egypt did not know about my plight? I banished Alexio's face from my mind and tried not to allow the desperation and longing for him to rise up to betray me. It would not do for a priestess of the Green Temple to have a husband. That information might put me in danger.

I moved my feet in the water to confuse the fish, and they scattered for a moment. "It is safe here, and I am not mistreated."

"Do you want to stay here and serve Isis? You have no memory of how you got here?"

Again, I heard the sound—not scraping, but scratching, coming from the other side of the wall. I tried not to stare over her shoulder, but I did quickly look just in case it was Paimu. There was no one there, but I could not see too well in the dark.

Maybe she was there. Waiting. I shivered as if somewhere someone had cursed me.

"No, I cannot remember," I told her honestly. "I never knew of this place until I woke up here."

"I see."

"I am not important enough to receive a visit from a queen. Why have you come?"

Her eyes widened at my directness. She had lovely eyes. Her other features were plain, but her eyes were like the dark eyes of a bird, ever attentive yet untrusting. As if everyone she met had a net in their hands and was ready to capture and consume her. Perhaps they were.

Poor Queen Tiye.

"I am told that there is no one greater at seeing than you. Nakmaa reports that you have extraordinary natural skills and can see great details in your visions. You have been very helpful to the priestesses here, but now I need something from you. I have many enemies, and my enemies are also your sister's enemies. Even if you do not care about me, I am sure you want to help her."

"My sister and I have different destinies," I said, giving her a sharp look. How surprising! I thought I had shed my old resentments toward Nefret. Perhaps a germ of hatred still remained. A subtle wind shifted in the garden, and the palm leaves clicked as they slapped into one another, confused by the change in the air.

"I do not speak of destinies but of loyalty and sisterhood."

"I see."

"Do you hate your sister?" she asked. "Do you believe she brought you here?"

Once I would have immediately answered, "Yes!" but that was before I murdered her treasure. Before I stole the queenship of our tribe from her. Before I betrayed her, first with Alexio and then with Farrah. Instead, I asked, "Do you have sisters, Queen Tiye? Have you never hated them?"

"I cannot remember their faces, but no, I never hated them."

Lying to herself. She hates everyone except for the son she lost.

Anxious to talk of something else and ready to be rid of her, I said, "Very well. I will help you. Let us look together. You are here, and the water is here. Let us try." I swept my hand across the surface, making ripples. I had never seen her in the water before, but it was worth a look. The idea of leaning over the hot flames for another moment made me sick to my stomach. The moon rose high above us now, and I could see its light bouncing back in the water. I smelled the white flowers, the kind that appeared only at night. Wide blooms waved around us, and thankfully, the mosquitoes had found somewhere else to congregate.

To my surprise, I immediately saw Queen Tiye. She was walking down a corridor with a baby in her arms, crooning to him quietly. *Was that a desert song? Ah, a lady of the Red Lands.* Then the scene changed, and she stood in a somber audience of people who surrounded a massive golden brazier. A man lay bound in the center of the altar, a sacrifice to some demanding god. I could see fear and regret in his dark eyes, but he did not cry out like a coward. I could feel his struggle. He wanted to cry out her name and tell her he loved her. Tell her that he would love her until the last flame licked away his flesh and bones, but he did not. He could see her on the edge of the brazier, weeping and crying over him. How strange he felt. He regretted drinking the water they gave him. It had made him weak and compliant. Then he saw the face of the man he had considered his friend, a man who was like a brother. It was Amenhotep!

I spoke nonstop, describing every detail revealed to me. As Queen Tiye had asked me, I held nothing back. I heard her gasp beside me. Without waiting for permission, she grabbed my hand, and I felt the vision transfer to her. I had never done this before, but I had heard it was possible.

"I see! I see!" She laughed for joy, but soon her face twisted. "No! This cannot be! Sitamen!" I strained to see but could not. "My daughter! Sitamen! No!" the tiny queen cried. To my surprise, she leaped to her feet and ran down the narrow path to wherever she intended to go. I did not have a chance to tell her that sometimes the seeing was in the past, and at other times it was the future. Or a possible future. One could never be sure.

I sighed and stood, dusting myself off. I felt extremely tired. Empty. I was sure I could sleep now. I had had enough excitement for one day.

Just as I turned to walk back to my quarters, I heard the scratching again. Feeling brave for only a second, I called in the direction of the noise.

"Now, spirit. Let us end this!"

I stared into the darkness toward the wall. I waited for a long while but saw nothing. I blinked against the blackness until I could see an arm, a pale, shining arm. It reached toward me from the wall. The small, grasping hand flexed its fingers as if to show me she was trying with all her might to reach me. To take her revenge. I walked toward the hand, closer and closer. My heart pounded and my skin crawled at the sight of the phantom struggling to reach me.

All my being hated every second of this experience, but I could not help but wonder what would happen if I reached out and touched the hand. Would she pull me away and take me to the Otherworld? What would happen to me? As I reached my hand toward hers, my fingers shook. How easy it would be to die now! I had nothing to live for anymore! I had cast off my child—lost my love—and was stolen from my tribe. There was nothing for me now.

Our fingers almost touched. As I got closer still, I heard whispers, whispers coaxing me to reach further, try harder, to come now...

"You, girl! Come away from there!" The guard's voice startled me out of my trance. I blinked at him and then at the wall. There was nothing there. The hand had disappeared, and the strange whispering had ceased. I stood before the wall alone, the only movement the short scrubby brush that swayed slightly in the breeze.

I had almost done it. I had almost surrendered to her. I owed her a debt, and she demanded payment, but I realized one of the goddess' servants had saved me.

"Yes," I said, smiling at him as the relief washed over me, "I will come away." The man stood holding his black spear and staring at me as if I were stupid. I did not care. I laughed at his expression. I had escaped death. The goddess had a plan for me—my work here in this world's realm was not done. I ran ahead of the guard and down the narrow corridor that led to my sleeping chambers.

Silently I climbed into my bed and lay there trying to control my breathing. She had come for me, to take me, but I had been saved! At least for now. I had another chance at life. Another chance to hope and dream that I would see the one I loved. Someday.

Before I fell asleep, I whispered in the dark, not to Isis but to my mother. "Watch over him, Mother. He is my husband and my love. Stay close to him, please."

With Magg snoring beside me, I fell asleep at last.

Chapter Nine

The New Sister—Nefertiti

I clapped and smiled at the sight of the collection of small animals led about on dainty silver chains by the children of the man who bowed before me. One animal, with a long neck and soft-looking fur, chattered away as he took his place on the small platform. A boy much younger than Paimu had been when she died led a similar animal to the opposite end of the toy. He made a whistling sound, and the two furry creatures—mongooses, they were called—began to bob up and down, making the tiny fulcrum move. I smiled at the children as they led the animals through their paces. When they had completed their performances, I tossed the animals the treats that the children provided me and gave the children handfuls of silver coins. Their dark eyes sparkled with excitement, and their father thanked me profusely.

"Thank you, lady queen," the children said, amazed at their collection of coins.

"You are quite welcome. That was a wonderful show. Seeing these animals reminds me of a story I once heard about a white elephant who stole a rare fruit but had to stand on his tiptoes to reach it." The children's eyes widened with delight, and big smiles appeared in anticipation of the story. I straightened my gown and was prepared to invite them to sit—it had been so long since I had told a story—but our meeting was interrupted by Menmet. I sighed sadly, knowing I could not spend more time with the children. I had other tasks to attend to, and the day had just begun.

For the first time in a long time, I would see Pah. My trusted spies (friends of Menmet) informed me that Pah had built quite a reputation for herself in the temple. She was recognized as a gifted seer now, and people from all over Thebes came to the Green Temple to hear her words. If that was true, then it would seem Tadukhipa's plan had not produced the desired effect. At least not for her. Perhaps Pah's experience had been real, and her goddess had saved her.

As the litter swung back and forth, I pulled the curtains back occasionally and waved at the gathering crowds who walked along beside us. Looking past their faces, I gazed up at the Green Temple of Isis in utter amazement. The glittering green columns shimmered in the sunshine. The columns and the building's façade were made of an unusual stone that had a streak of gold throughout it. I could see why people from around the world came to see this temple. Although I rarely came here, the sight of it still took my breath away. And to think Pah lived here now.

As a courtesy to me, and to erase any doubts about my heritage, Tiye had quietly recognized Pah as a daughter of Isis. Technically she was a royal and entitled to all the benefits of her status. I sent her gifts and messages, hoping to measure her feelings for me before I arrived, but she had not responded.

A green-robed priestess greeted me on the steps and politely took me to an empty hall that led to an area where Pah and I could visit privately. Without a word, the priestess left me standing in the open room, and I waited nervously for my sister.

I heard her bare feet slapping on the stones as she approached. Pah's face was so pale it glowed, and she appeared gaunter than I had ever seen her. She looked so much older than her true seasons. Before all this, before Fate had had her way with us, looking upon her was like looking in a mirror. Even now our eyes remained the same, only mine were lined with kohl applied by Menmet's deft hand. It was an ironic twist considering how much I had hated Egypt, and she had wanted to embrace it. Yet now I represented the Two Lands in the most supreme way possible.

Pah's short red hair gleamed in the light. The gown she wore was too large for her thin figure, as if it were not made for her at all but for a giant. The sleeves were far too large, and it lacked any adornment. She did not wear the clothing I sent her or anything fine.

When last I saw my sister, she spoke to the invisible world and screamed and cried at random. Now here she was, quiet and composed, without a trace of her former confidence or haughtiness. Before I left Zerzura, Leela seemed convinced that Pah carried a child, but if she were pregnant, she should be showing by now, as I was. I had long decided I would offer to care for her child since she could not do so here at the temple, but now that point was moot.

"I cast it out after I arrived here," she answered my unspoken question. "It was my choice, sister. No one forced me."

"Why would you do that? Children are our treasures!" The words fell from my lips before I could stop them. What a foolish thing to say to someone who had endured what Pah had. How could I pass judgment on her?

She did not rebuke me or defend herself. "I am sorry about the child," she said in a low voice, her tired eyes never leaving mine. I could hear the heartbreak in her voice.

"I understand. Truly, I do. I have no right to tell you what to do."

She shook her head sadly. "No, sister. You misunderstand me. It is your treasure I speak of. The girl—Paimu. What I did to her. I robbed you of her love and took her life when it was not mine to take. The deed weighs on me, and I am sorry for it."

I never thought to hear such a confession. A sob of surprise and pain escaped me as Paimu's face came unbidden to my mind's eye. I had put her away in my mind, unwilling to conjure up her sweet face, her cheerful laughter, and playful spirit. I felt guilty for leaving her memory behind so easily. She had brought joy to my lonely life, as I hoped I had brought to hers.

"Why, Pah? Why did you do it? She was just a child and no threat to you." My voice rose and echoed through the initiates' hall, surprising the temple guards and my companions who waited for me in the hallway. Menmet could not enter this place. Only the servants or the daughters of Isis could enter here. Whatever happened here, we were by ourselves except for the onlookers' watchful eyes.

Pah's expression lacked her typical disdain and contempt. That had vanished like her haughty looks. Regret took its place. "Nothing I can say will satisfy your need to understand, for I myself do not understand why I did it." Her pretty voice sounded empty of hope. "For a long time, I could not think clearly—my mind was a hateful playground. It was as if a wrathful spirit lived inside me and would not go away. No matter how my heart broke, how much I wanted to reach out to someone, I could not. I did not seek Paimu, but when she crossed my path that morning, I killed her. I do not even know why I carried the knife with me. I am sorry for that. With all my heart and soul, I am sorry."

"I did not want to believe it, but now that I hear it from your lips, I know that it is true."

"Why have you come here, Nefret?"

"I wanted to...I had to see you. I had to tell you that it was not my idea to bring you here." I dropped my voice to a whisper and said quickly, "I believe my adversary, Tadukhipa, organized your abduction, but I do not know why. Can you identify your captors so that I can question them? I need to know what she has planned."

"Ah, I see."

"What is it you see?" I asked her.

"I see the fires of ambition burning in you, Nefret. I know those fires. They will burn you up if you allow them to."

"You are wrong, sister. I am trying to help you. How did you get here?"

"I cannot remember. I have tried." Suddenly she stepped toward me and said, "Please, Nefret. Let me go home. Home to Alexio. You have your husband. You are queen now. Please let me go."

"I did not bring you here, Pah. The Great Queen's steward, Huya, has been investigating your case. He says that you must have a special dispensation from the priestess here before you can go and that she is loath to release you."

"Why? Why won't they let me go? I want to go home."

"You have been looking in the fire and water. You have seen what they cannot. As it always is, the one who can't see wants to see more. Since you have proved you have skills and can see visions, they do not want to release you."

"What must I do, Nefret? I want to go home. I had thought I would never leave. You did not come to me when I asked for you, but now I feel hope that I will escape. You will let me go, won't you? You are queen now! You can do this!"

"I am trying, Pah. You must make it easier, though. Stop sharing the visions. When people ask you to see, tell them you cannot. Maybe then Nakmaa will release you."

"You want me to lie?"

I took her hands. They were cool to the touch and almost lifeless. "If you want to go home, you are going to have to stop looking into the fire and water. When Pharaoh returns to Thebes, I will ask him to intercede for you. Until then, no more visions, Pah."

She sighed, and it was a hopeless sound. "It is Alexio, isn't it? You still love him."

In a whisper, I tried to reassure her, "I regret how I left things with him, but I love my husband. I love Amenhotep like I have never loved anyone. I swear to you, Pah. I did not bring you here, nor am I keeping you from Alexio. I will try to help you, but do as I ask."

"Paimu. The girl," she whispered back. With fearful eyes, she scanned the room. Seeing no one, she whispered again, "She dogs my steps, sister. I see her lingering outside the gate when the sun comes up and when it goes down. She has not breached the walls yet, but sometimes when I dive deep into the water she is there, waiting for me. I think she will drown me if she can. Sometimes when I look into the fire, her face appears, her eyes like flames of hatred. She wants her life back, and I cannot give it to her." She stepped back quickly and withdrew her hand as if mine were two snakes. "Did you bring her here? Is that why you came? You and Farrah?"

"Paimu is dead, Pah. And in death or life, she would never harm you. What you see is your own guilt."

"So you say, but you do not see like I can. I see them both."

"Farrah? Why would she come to Egypt?" I tried to tease her to keep her mind from dwelling on her evil deeds. She pulled away from me and gave me a wide-eyed stare. Her figure appeared so small as she stood in the middle of the sparse room, the looming stone statue of Isis behind her, a basin of water to the left of it, a brazier of fire on the right. She did not belong here, but I did not know what to do to help her. I needed more information—proof that Tadukhipa had arranged her appointment here, against her will. What did my enemy have planned for my sister and me?

With raw fierceness, she said, "I killed Farrah, and I will not deny it. Nor do I regret it. She deserved to die. She betrayed Mother and left her to die in the desert. She betrayed you too, Nefret, whether you believe me or not. If she were standing before me now, I would kill her again. A hundred times over!"

"Pah, calm down! Farrah would harm no one! All she ever wanted to do was lead us home to Zerzura."

"Well then, why didn't she lead us home? I will tell you why—because she could not. Farrah did not remember the way, and she could not rely on the sight to lead her. She murdered an innocent, our mother, and her crime cost her. The gods saw fit to take her visions from her. The Old One lied to us when she said she could see. She saw nothing but shadows. It was I who saw!"

"But you have taken two lives, Pah, and you see."

Her lovely eyes narrowed as she considered my words. She stepped toward me out of the shadow of the hovering Isis. She did not lash out at me or show frustration with what she used to call my stupidity. Her eyes swept me up and down as if she were seeing me in a new light. It made me uncomfortable, but I did not shrink from her gaze. Let her look at me if she wanted to! I was the Queen of Egypt—Queen Nefertiti! All our lives, my sister had done only what was beneficial for her, but I had chosen another route and had done what was right for the tribe. Who was she to judge me?

Somewhere in another room, I heard bells tinkling and hands clapping. These were likely signs that worship was about to begin, but Pah made no move to leave me. She continued her silent appraisal and then spoke with renewed clarity.

"I believed their lies when they told me that I was the better mekhma, the better leader. They knew how jealous I was, how unreasonable were my thoughts! You were right. We should have reigned together and dared anyone to stand against us. I cannot go back and change what I have done, but I can help you now. Help me leave here, and I will look for you—only you. I swear it."

My insides melted like wax. I never imagined hearing these words from my sister, and now that I heard them, I barely trusted myself to believe them. If only we could go back and change things. If only we could go back and rule together and defeat the Kiffians without making deals with Egypt. But things had changed. I loved Amenhotep, and even if I could change my position in life, I would never leave him. I never wanted to be away from him.

"My husband and I worship the Aten. We do not seek visions of the future. We will build a new Egypt, one free from the oppression of the priests and priestesses. I cannot imagine Isis would like me too well for it."

"When I look at you, I see the shining one—yes, a Shining Man. He is near you now. I can see his image behind you, sister."

I gasped in surprise. I had never shared with her my experiences with the Shining Man. How could she know of him? I was tempted to look behind me, so steady and powerful was her gaze, but I did not.

She wrapped her arms around me, but I stiffened. She whispered in my ear, "Forgive me, Nefret."

Try as I might, I could not resist her embrace for long, and I hugged her back. Being the Queen of Egypt I had learned a few things from Queen Tiye, such as not letting emotions compromise you in any situation, but at this moment, I did not care about those lessons. I heard the tinkling of the bells again and saw a priestess waiting in the opposite doorway. She whispered a word in a language I did not understand, but evidently Pah did.

My sister stepped back, squeezing my hands reassuringly. "I must go now. The goddess calls me. Do not forget my promise."

"I will come to see you again soon. Remember what I told you." I smiled at her, thankful for this happy moment. These had been too few.

She smiled back, but her expression quickly changed. A frown crept upon her brow, and her lips pursed in serious thought. "Sister! You have more than one enemy. Trust no one."

Before I could inquire of her further, Pah took the hand of the priestess beside her, and the two disappeared down the corridor. I stood staring after her, wondering about her words, but I did not have time to linger in the Green Temple. My court—Amenhotep's court—waited for my attention. Menmet shuffled her feet impatiently, and I went to her. We rode back to the palace in silence. I was thankful that she did not ply me with questions, for I knew she was curious. Menmet was always curious. Queen Tiye's recent warnings rang in my ears: *She is Heby's daughter and a spy. Do not be a fool, Nefertiti!*

I focused on my next task, administering justice in Thebes. I had to focus on the people who came before me. I remembered Amenhotep's admonition. "Make the people love you, my queen. Let them see you as a good queen. Win their hearts!"

Oh, Amenhotep! When will you come home to me?

As I prepared for attendance at court, I was delighted to see a stack of new gifts waiting for me in my chambers. Amenhotep and I had had barely any correspondence in the past few weeks, but he had faithfully sent me gift after gift. Each one I was sure had some special meaning that he wished to convey to me. I spent many a night pondering them, touching them. Menmet clapped her hands joyfully at the sight. I loved her enthusiasm. She celebrated when I celebrated, cried when I cried. Wasn't that the definition of a friend? A sister? She handed me a box from the top of the stack. It was wrapped in blue cloth and had an exquisite silver ribbon tying it together. I pulled the ribbon and released the lid from the top. Inside was an elegant golden brooch in the shape of the sun, with a crown that rested on the top. I reached out to pick it up, but Menmet stopped me.

"My queen! Do not touch that!" She swatted my hands as if I were a child.

"What is the matter with you?" I shouted. If the Great Queen Tiye had seen her do such a thing, she would have put her in irons. I could not blame her. If she was too familiar, it was my own fault.

"That is the crowned sun! A Hittite symbol. This must be from Tadukhipa, not Amenhotep. Knowing her, the thing is dipped in poison or covered in curses. At the very least, she is trying to send you a message."

"Perhaps," I said absently as I examined the item without touching it. I knew what the message was, but I did not share my observations. Pah had warned me that I had more than one enemy. I did not want to believe it could be Menmet, but as I had learned of late, anything was possible in Egypt's courts.

I called Harwa to me for answers. "Who brought these gifts in here? Where did this one come from?"

The old eunuch examined the stack of boxes and crates and said, "All these came from our Pharaoh. But this one, I do not know. It was not here before, my queen."

"That means someone brought it here without anyone's notice?"

Harwa frowned at the thought and began to call together those who had been nearby to see what they had observed. I did not wait for the results of his investigation.

I stared at the brooch as I chewed my lip. We had heard quite a bit lately about Tadukhipa's growing power. People whispered that her sun rose as mine faded. I had even heard that she was pregnant and that Amenhotep had made his final decision. He would make Tadukhipa the Great Queen at last, they said. Even my court had become emptier during his absence. Each day, it was the same. In the mornings I took reports from our kenbet, a class of leaders who led specific districts on our behalf. These were mostly men from the noble class, but there were also common men amongst this esteemed group. I listened as patiently as I could to their concerns about slaves, water and grain. Sometimes I offered advice, but most of the time I simply listened as the scribes wrote down the complaints. In the afternoons, I heard cases selected from the domestic courts by my advisers. This was not typical behavior for a queen or any royal, but I had taken Amenhotep's instructions seriously.

"Let the people see that you love them! Lead them, Nefertiti."

What if none of that mattered now? What if Amenhotep had truly made his decision? According to whispers, I should go ahead and pack my belongings now and move into the Royal Harem. But I refused to leave the palace.

"Harwa, listen to me. Do not worry about that now. If it is indeed a gift from my sister, Queen Tadukhipa, I must wear it. But I do not think anyone wears brooches at the moment. They have gone out of fashion, I am afraid. Take this brooch and have it hammered into a crown. Leave its shape—I want her to be able to recognize it when she sees me, so she knows how much I appreciate her gift. I want it ready for her return to demonstrate my gratitude."

Harwa grinned, showing his even smile. He had the perfect teeth of a child and pleasant brown eyes. I instantly trusted him when I met him, but I was also glad that he was on my side. He could be as devious as Queen Tiye and her steward, Huya. Nobody outsmarted those two. "Should we add your falcon crest to the center spire?"

"Harwa, you read my mind."

Amenhotep had invited me here, and here I planned to stay.

Chapter Ten

The Visitors—Nefertiti

The official court was located at the front of the palace. I had to walk downstairs and down the length of the main corridor to access it. As I made the trip, I remembered to keep my face a serene mask, just as Tiye taught me. Her tutelage had been invaluable these past few weeks. Although she was impatient with me and sometimes unkind, she had a shrewdness that I envied. She saw problems long before I did, and during those first days in the court she had helped me navigate the formalities without failure. Today I entered the court without her and heard the hush fall upon the waiting crowd. I walked steadily up the back of the dais and stood before the throne.

Trusted members of my court brought me a few cases each day, and lately, I began noticing a pattern. More and more of these cases involved children and the priests of Amun. What they were doing was wrong—taking them from their parents, sacrificing them, burning them—and I secretly vowed to stop their horrific rituals and practices. Menmet had been my partner in this.

The throne attendants lifted my heavy robes. I glanced over to see that scribes were waiting with ink and papyrus, ready to make my words the law of the land. I took my seat upon my husband's throne, and the people rose from their bowed positions in expectation. Even after all these weeks, almost months, it was still a humbling sight to me. I refused to take the privilege for granted. The gold fabric had been draped smoothly over the back and across the dais by the experienced hands of the attendants. I held the heavy brass crook and flail in my hands. The weight seemed easier to manage now. At least, I thought, the regular courtiers appeared less shocked when I sat in Amenhotep's place. I hoped that the news of my work here had reached his ears.

"The people need to see you as Queen of Upper and Lower Egypt. Lead them, my wife."

His confidence in me gave me strength, but it did little to put my heart at ease. He was, after all, in the arms of Queen Tadukhipa even now. I had hotly contested this arrangement, but after a visit from the Hittite-Mitanni king, I could hardly stand in my husband's way. If we wanted peace with the Hittites, Amenhotep would have to honor the marriage put in place by his father.

How strange these Egyptians were! Sons inheriting wives, concubines, and harems. It was a strange thing indeed, but my husband assured me his heart remained with me. Like so many things in my life, this matter was out of my control. I would make the best of it. And as Tiye often reminded me, the true prize had not yet been won. My rule these many weeks was very likely a test, Tiye had whispered to me during our evening meal last night.

Another test in a life of testing.

I thought about her other words, warnings to me. "Do not trust her. Even at this distance. She has her monsters here. There is one of them." She had pointed at Menmet, who was busy preparing a tray of fresh fruit for us.

I had not argued with her, for it would have done no good. Of course, Queen Tiye refused to eat anything taken from Menmet's hand. Menmet noticed the slight, I could see, but she kept her place.

Queen Tiye hated Tadukhipa beyond reason, almost as much as she hated the priests of Amun. In truth, she seemed to have little love for anyone except her dead husband and her son Thutmose and, of course, Pharaoh Amenhotep. Poor Sitamen was ever lost in the shadows.

Menmet informed me that more royal visitors had come to the Theban court that morning, ready to pay homage to Pharaoh and

Queen Nefertiti. I sat up stiffly as Harwa bowed toward me. With a clap of his hands, the outer doors opened, and I blinked against the sunlight that poured in through the throne room. My wig itched and my stomach rumbled, but I kept my face like stone as the small contingent approached me.

From the moment he stepped into the inner court, I recognized him. Alexio! Shaggy dark hair hung about his shoulders, and he wore a clean blue tunic, leather leggings, and sandals. Beside Alexio were a few others: Biel, the young man I had met at Zerzura, had now grown even taller, and I could see that Horemheb had returned to Egypt. I anxiously awaited his report from home.

I felt the eyes of the court upon me, and I forced myself to breathe normally as the group approached. I wondered if any of them knew who this man was who came before my throne. Who he used to be to me? *My husband.* Alexio had not changed—he looked a little older, a little unhappier. He showed no excitement at seeing me, nor did I expect any. I had betrayed him at the highest level. I had taken an oath under the stars, swearing to love him with my mind, body, and soul always and call him mine forever. Then I'd sent him away in a moment of anger. I did not deserve him.

I listened respectfully as Harwa announced the leaders of the Meshwesh. "Horemheb, friend of Egypt, brings gifts of turquoise to Pharaoh and his queen, Nefertiti. May he present them?" I nodded my permission, careful to keep my movements smooth and easy so as not to disturb the scented wig and crown that rested uneasily on my head.

Horemheb stepped forward stiffly. I could see that age was beginning to take its toll on him. I wondered about my father, but I would question my uncle later. For now, I focused on the formalities. He knelt on one knee as he held open a round cedar chest full of bits of turquoise jewelry. It was not a fine prize—Horemheb was aware it was not as fine as the gifts the Hittites and Cushites offered—but I knew it was the tribe's best. The Meshwesh were not a stingy people. I thanked them for their kind gifts to Pharaoh.

"Welcome, my father's people," I said warmly. There could be only one reason why they were here—to see their mekhma and, if possible, bring her home. Sadly, I understood that although I was the mekhma who had saved them, brought them back to Zerzura, raised them to a seat of respect in Egypt, I was not the one they came to rescue.

I would never be rescued. My fate was sealed. I was no longer a Desert Queen but the Queen of all Egypt.

With my head held high, I said, "It would please me greatly if you would dine with me this evening. I would like very much to hear the latest news from the White City."

"Thank you, Queen Nefertiti. You do us great honor." Before they could say anything else, I gave a long nod of dismissal. Alexio lingered, likely ready to make his feelings known, but Horemheb led him away by his elbow.

Harwa watched with some concern. I had promised him I would dine with the Grecians this evening, and perhaps I would. It was not unheard of to host two banquets at one time. As Tiye told me, I need not explain myself to the servants, neither the high ones nor the low ones. "And they are all your servants," she added with authority.

After the whispers settled, we welcomed the next assembly as they approached my throne. There would be no reports today, thankfully. No endless complaints from leaders. Receiving guests to court was much easier, or so I first believed. I quickly learned that each nation had its own greetings and expectations. Harwa sometimes spent hours preparing me for the occasion. "Do not stare at his eye patch," he had told me when Cervantes came to court. Another time, he had instructed me, "Speak to the women first. They take great offense if they are not recognized, and they are the true power in Persia. Also do not mention any other nations when speaking to them. We are in negotiations for access to some of their harbors this winter. They are very jealous for Egypt's attention."

Tiye had been correct. Harwa had become invaluable to me. He knew everyone and everything. What he did not know, Menmet knew. I felt much more confident than I had just a few weeks ago, having them by my side. I watched respectfully as an assembly of Grecians walked toward me. I felt a great curiosity about these people, as they were my relatives. The Egyptians had great love for them, but I had seen only a few Grecians during my years in the Red Lands. I had my mother's red hair, but most of my mother's people had blonde or light brown hair with bronze skin and light-colored eyes, all features Egyptians regarded as unusual and attractive. The approaching assembly paused at a respectful distance and waited for Harwa to recognize them.

"Queen Nefertiti, may I present to you Ianos, Kallias, and Sophos, ambassadors from King Orestes. I think they have gifts for you, lady queen." I studied them as they approached. They were attractive, but most ambassadors were since they were supposedly representative of their monarchs. Each was tall, much taller than I, but not as tall as Amenhotep. They wore short-sleeved tunics that were cinched at the waist with beautifully worked leather belts. As was the tradition for court, they did not carry weapons, but I could see an empty scabbard on the hip of the man in the middle. He seemed the most striking to me. None wore beards, and they kept their hair short in the soldier's fashion. They had muscular arms and legs, although Ianos, who appeared to be the oldest, had skinny legs like my uncle.

"They are welcome here, Harwa. Welcome to the court of Amenhotep, ambassadors. I am sure Pharaoh will be saddened to know that he missed your visit, but perhaps you will come again when he returns."

My answer pleased them, and they bowed graciously. One of them said to me, "Greetings, Queen Nefertiti. I am Kallias, the son of

Alistair, the brother of Princess Kadeema. I am happy to finally meet you. It is a meeting that is long overdue, I think."

I could not help but flash a smile at the man. He had a handsome face, but unlike many handsome faces, he did not have a haughty look or way about him. Kallias wore no jewelry but had an elegant demeanor that proved his noble birth. "Yes, I agree. Welcome to Thebes, Kallias. Have you been here before?"

"No, this is my first visit to Pharaoh's city."

"Then perhaps you and the other ambassadors will join me for a tour of my husband's gardens after I greet all my guests. I would like to hear about Grecia and Kadeema's homeland."

Kallias appeared enormously pleased by my offer. "Nothing would give us more pleasure, Queen Nefertiti. We are at your service. We have a gift for you. May I present it?" I ignored Harwa's questioning look and waved Kallias forward. He walked up the first three steps of the dais until he heard the throne room guards come to attention. Stopping immediately, he knelt on the marble step and opened a small box that was no bigger than my hand. Inside was the largest, shiniest pearl I had ever seen, and I had seen many since my arrival in Thebes. It was strung on a thin golden chain.

In a soft voice, Kallias said, "This pearl comes from the harbor of Illeas, the home of Kadeema. It is a rare jewel. Our king sends the gift with his warmest greetings."

"I can see that it is remarkable," I said with honest admiration. "May I touch it?"

"It is yours, Queen Nefertiti."

I rose from my throne, ignoring the gasps of the people. It was a rare thing to see Pharaoh rise from his throne, except during special occasions. But then again, I was not Pharaoh. I had forgotten the rules, but I made no apologies to anyone. The gift moved me.

I took the pearl in my hand and slid it up and down the chain, examining the workmanship. "Rise, Kallias. Tell King Orestes that I gladly accept his gift and welcome his friendship. You are all welcome at court. Please remain as my esteemed guests." He stepped down off the dais, and together the three of them bowed again. I heard a noise from the waiting gallery. Feeling a little irritated at the interruption, I kept my voice cool. "Ah, I see more guests have arrived. You may stay if you like." They stepped to the side, and I clutched the pearl in my hand as I took my seat.

At least a dozen dark-headed men wearing rich leather armor over brightly colored tunics had gathered. My guards were busy unburdening the visitors of their weapons. It was common knowledge that visitors to court did not bring their weapons with them, so I wondered at the meaning of this. Then they walked toward me, almost marching in time. They stomped across the floor in heavy boots, their long hair flowing behind them. Their fierce, narrow eyes never shifted from me, nor my own eyes from them.

Hittites! Kinsmen of Tadukhipa, no doubt. Let us see how this goes.

Before Harwa could scramble to the front of the dais, the men presented themselves to me. They held their heads high and appraised me unashamedly as they waited impatiently for the formalities to end. Harwa did not name all the Hittites, only one. His name was Tishratta, and I knew it was a name I would always remember.

He was very dark but not black like the men from the south. His skin was almost a strange green color. Then I realized it was painted, and what wasn't painted was covered with tattoos. I made myself focus on his face and not his painted arms. His black eyes were lined with kohl, which made them look even darker. His hair was so long that the top of it was pulled back from his face with a sturdy-looking leather thong. Like Tadukhipa, he had few smiles for the people around him, assuming that everyone knew who he was and that he commanded their respect. As Harwa began to recite the many titles of King Tishratta, I stood for the second time today.

"King Tishratta, I am surprised to see you here. As you know, Queen Tadukhipa is touring the Nile with my husband and having a memorable time, from what I am told. Did you know she sent me a lovely gift today? Can you guess what it is?"

He did not answer at first, but as the court began to whisper, I supposed he felt compelled to do so. "I am not good at guessing games, Queen Nefertiti. Speak what is on your mind."

Looking down at him with a smile, I said, "A lovely brooch in the shape of the sun with a crown atop it. Can you interpret it for me? Why would she give me such a gift? As lovely as it is, I cannot wear it, not unless I want to offend my husband. For surely the crowned sun is the symbol of the Hittite empire. Was she suggesting you take me to wife, King Tishratta?" The crowd whispered and pointed at the king and his retinue. They were as surprised as he was to hear my words. "No. That must be wrong because I am the wife of the Egyptian Pharaoh, a great and generous king who has chosen both Tadukhipa and me as wife. I have abandoned my people and claimed Egypt as my own. Hasn't my sister-wife done the same?"

"She has. What are you accusing her of, Queen Nefertiti?" I could see his jaw clench and his fist curl.

Without moving my head, I glanced at Harwa, whose eyes reminded me to tread lightly. I replied, "Merely bad judgment. I have no specific accusation against her. I am simply asking about the nature of her curious gift. I do not understand it. I am sure sweet Tadukhipa had some kind gesture in mind, but since I cannot fathom it, I have decided to accept her gift anyway. My steward Harwa has delivered the brooch into my jeweler's hands. He will make sure it is fit for a queen of Egypt. Please stay for my banquet this evening so you can see the gift she gave me. Thank you for attending me today."

I rose from the dais, leaving him standing stupidly before the throne. I walked out of the court, smiling generously at my people and stopping to accept their bows of devotion and blessings.

Once we left the long court processional, with the Hittites staring open-mouthed at our backs, Harwa found me and whispered, "My queen, what will Pharaoh say about this? I am sure he will hear about it. You have only given them reason to hate you more."

"Do you think it will come back to bite me?"

Harwa sighed but smiled. "Of course it will, but we'll be ready for them. It sounds to me like tonight's banquet will be interesting indeed. Hittites, Grecians, and Meshwesh together?"

"Why not? We are Egypt, the most civilized nation in the world. If any of our guests have a problem with one another, it is their problem to have. Make sure the gift is ready for me to wear by tonight, Harwa."

"It shall be done, my queen."

"Tell Menmet to come to me."

I walked back up the staircase with my minor servants a safe distance behind me. I did not invite them to talk to me, although I knew that for many, it would have been the dream of a lifetime. I was not feeling so generous at the moment. I had to think. If Queen Tiye had been there, what would she have said? Would she have even received them? She would have scolded me for letting my feelings get the better of me, but I think she would have agreed with my decision. Since Tadukhipa was openly challenging me for the title of Great Wife, I must return the favor. I pushed the door open to my chambers and was surprised to see a young girl waiting for me. She was on her knees, folding scarves. She wore a worn purple gown and a robe of blue. I could see right away that she was Meshwesh.

"Who are you? How did you get in here?"

"I am Sunami. I was sent here by your uncle Horemheb, the man we call Omel. I am to be in your court, mekhma Nefret. Oh, excuse me, Queen Nefertiti!"

Hearing a voice from home delighted my soul, especially at this moment when my hands and confidence were shaking. "Welcome then, Sunami. Stand. Let me look at you."

She stood and raised her face slowly. As she did, I could see she was beautiful. She had an angular face, large luminous eyes the color of mist, and short bangs with long black hair. Ah, she had been one of Farrah's acolytes. Only those women let their tresses grow to such lengths. "You look familiar to me. Have we met?" I saw something flash in those expressive eyes, but I did not know her well enough to decipher it. Fear, perhaps? Fear that I would reject her? "You do not have to be afraid of me. I do not eat children or young women, Sunami."

"We have never met, Mekhma, I mean, Queen Nefertiti, but I have seen you many times at Timia and at Zerzura."

"Ziza! That is who you favor! Is everything all right with the girl?"

"Oh, yes, Ziza is my little cousin. All is well. She is growing and sends her love to you."

I clapped my hands in delight and hugged her as if she were an old friend. About that time, Menmet bounced into the room, ready to serve me. "Never mind, Menmet. Meet Sunami, my new maidservant. You must show her how to dress. Perhaps we can save her hair and not cut it, but I am not sure it can be avoided, Sunami."

"I will be happy to cut my hair to serve you, Queen Nefertiti."

"We will worry about that later. Right now, I need your help choosing clothing for tonight. Menmet is always wanting to show off my body in these sheer robes, but as you can see, I have a big belly now. I cannot walk around with my breasts exposed." Menmet pouted at my teasing words.

"No, indeed. You are Queen of Egypt. You cannot do such things. Let Sunami help you, sweet queen."

Menmet whispered in my ear, "There is a man who says he must meet with you privately." Even more quietly, she said, "It is Alexio, lady queen."

I drew back as if she had bitten me. "What?" She did not speak again but nodded her affirmation. I tried to keep my composure. "Very well. Sunami, you stay here and find something blue for me to wear. The

Grecians were wearing blue. I think it is important to show where my allegiance lies, at least today. I will return soon."

She smiled, but there was no warmth in it. In fact, my skin felt clammy at the sight of it. I waved my hand dismissively and left her standing in my rooms alone.

I followed Menmet down to my private gardens and could see Alexio pacing there. "Please, Menmet. Stay with me. He and I cannot be alone together. Also, help me take off my robe. This heat is unbearable."

"Should I ask why?"

"You should not." I knew she loved me. How could I think of replacing her? Tiye had been wrong about her. *Stop thinking about this right now, Nefret. You have bigger things to think about.* There was danger afoot throughout my palace.

I walked out into the sunlight and stood patiently, waiting for Alexio to notice me. I learned this trick from Queen Tiye, who loved to surprise people. She moved like Lady Silence herself. And, she bragged once, she learned a great deal just by standing like a statue.

"Oh, Nefret. You came."

"This is Queen Nefertiti, sir. Please call her by her proper name since it is illegal to do otherwise."

"Forgive me, madam. May we speak in private, Queen Nefertiti? I have a boon to ask of you."

"You can speak freely in front of Menmet. She is my most trusted adviser."

"Sit, lady. I will attend you. Do you want water or wine?"

"Water, please, Menmet."

We waited as she poured us a drink. I sat at the table and invited Alexio to sit with me. He took a drink and looked around him nervously. "It is I, Alexio. Your friend and countryman. Please do not feel afraid here." He looked at me, and I felt the familiar tug at my heart. He continued, "It's just that there are things I would say to you that I..."

"Speak your mind, Alexio hap Omel." I said the words pleasantly but rubbed my stomach protectively. He swallowed and got the message. I no longer belonged to him. I was Pharaoh's wife.

"I came to plead for the release of my wife, Pah hap Semkah, your sister. I know you do not believe me, or maybe you will understand this now, now that you are so happy with your Pharaoh. I love her. I think I always did. I do not know why it took me so long to realize that, but she needs me, and I need her, Nefret. I mean, please, Queen Nefertiti, let her go. I do not know why she is being held in the temple, but you of all people should know that Pah is not well. Please set her free and send her home where she will be cared for by people who know and love her." He spoke so passionately and suddenly that it surprised me. He added in a low voice, "If you ever loved me or cared for me, please, send her back to me."

I could see the tears in his eyes, and it was a strange thing to see. I wanted to slap him. Scream at him. Beg him to at least want me, but I did none of those things. I did not love him, not like I loved Amenhotep. Why was I so resistant to his request?

"*I* have not arrested her. *I* did not bring her here. In fact, Pah cannot remember who brought her, nor can she tell us why. But you may visit her. There is an investigation into this matter, but I do not know who arranged this. And I cannot fathom why someone would have sent her to the Green Temple. However, it is more complicated now. She is a proven seer, and her skills have made her a valuable asset to the priestesses there. And, of course, to Isis. I have a suspicion that they might release Pah at a price. They will lose money if she leaves. And more than anything, these temple priests and priestesses here value money. It is something my husband and I hope to change during our reign."

He looked at me with a questioning expression. "So, you are happy? You want to be with—I mean, in Thebes?"

Without thinking, I leaned forward and took his hand in mine. I whispered to him, uncaring who saw me, "Fate led me away, and I cannot resist my destiny. I am sorry, Alexio."

"I hated you when you left."

"I know."

"Those were lies, Nefr—Nefertiti. And you believed them. You should have believed *me*. You should have let me stay by your side."

"And if I had? How could I have ever released you? But now I know you love Pah. That is good."

He had something else to say, but he did not say it, and I did not prompt him to speak his mind. Some things did not need to be and should not be said.

"Go to the temple tomorrow, Alexio. I will arrange for you to visit your wife. There is a small area where sometimes priestesses are afforded visits from family members, but do not tell them you are her husband. I am sure they would not welcome you if they knew. The priestesses of Isis are all unmarried. Talk to her. Find out what you can. Did she take an oath? If she did, it will be more difficult to remove her from the temple, but I would not say it is impossible. I will pay for her release since she did not willingly enter the temple herself. Help her remember, Alexio. Send Horemheb to me tomorrow, and we will meet with Nakmaa, the High Priestess at the Isis temple. Horemheb has charm with women, and she seems like one who enjoys being charmed."

Alexio wiped sudden tears from his eyes. "And you don't hate me?"

"How could I? I should be asking you that question."

"I wish you a house full of children, my friend," he said, gesturing toward my belly.

"And you, Alexio." As we rose from the table, he was all smiles. He hugged me impetuously, and I did not stop him even though Menmet frowned disapprovingly. Soon he was gone, and I watched him leave knowing that would likely be the last time I saw him. I sighed, but it was not a regretful sigh. More an appreciation that a part of my life was officially over. No more days swimming aimlessly in the pool at Timia. No more climbing trees with my treasures or eating grapes from Alexio's hand. Everything was different, and it always would be.

I heard the bells chime, sounding the time throughout the palace. "Oh, no! I need to bathe and dress. Let's go, Menmet."

She took my hand, and we ran up the stairs together. I felt free. Freer than I had in a long time. Laughing at myself trying to race with my ball of a belly, I swung open the doors and froze in my tracks. Hanging from the golden rail that led to the top level of my apartment was a body. The body of Sunami! She was obviously dead, having been stabbed multiple times. I felt nausea rise in my belly, and I heard a strange sound. It was a woman's voice, extremely loud, and the enunciations were all wrong.

"Please, mekhma. I only help." In my surprise, I had not noticed the second body on the floor. It was Mina, Farrah's acolyte.

"Murderer!" Menmet screamed at her.

"No! Stop, Menmet!" Before I could get hold of her, the guards were in the rooms. They immediately cut down the body and tried to assess the danger. "No, leave the woman alone. There is no danger here. Please. Just give me a minute." I sat on the floor next to Mina. I could see that she too had slash marks along her arms and chest, and some were very vicious and deep. "What happened, my friend? Who did this to you?"

"I help," she yelled.

"Mina, speak softly now. You do not have to yell. Save your air."

"Astora!" she yelled again, and then I saw her jaw go slack, and her eyes roll up to something I could not see.

"Astora? Mina! Come back to me! Where is Astora?"

Menmet screamed in surprise as she knelt by the body of my new servant. "Queen Nefertiti! This is not Sunami! Who is this?"

"What do you mean? She is in Sunami's clothing. Who else could it be?"

The guards had removed the body and laid it on the floor. I pushed back the long hair and could plainly see that it was much shorter now. The face became clearer, and the last of the illusion faded. There was the face of Astora, the wife of Horemheb. She had fresh tattoos on her face, and her eyes were dead. Wondering who else was dead here, I ran up the last flight of stairs and looked around my bedchambers. There were no other bodies, but all my gowns had been slashed to pieces with the same knife that appeared to have been used on Astora. Who had done this? Astora/Sunami? Or maybe Mina? I could not fathom it. I sat on the bed and cried as my servants began cleaning my chambers.

Oh, Amenhotep! Come home soon! Death is all around me!

Chapter Eleven

Twisting Snakes—Pah

Never do I dream, except for last night. Then she came to me like an angry tiger, growling with snarling teeth and reaching, evil claws. She wanted to take from me what I took from her. She said nothing, just slashed at me. I felt the cuts, one after the other. I felt the blood pouring from my wounds. I fell to my knees, unable to fend off her cruel slices. I raised my outstretched hand to protect my face. I waited for the death strike, perhaps at my throat, but it did not come. The awful tearing, the painful slices ceased.

Crying and begging for my miserable life, I slowly lifted my head.

The tiger with Paimu's face had disappeared. Now it was the girl, her hair disheveled and dirty with desert sand, her tunic stained with dark blood and her eyes...black and lifeless. They peered into my soul.

Her mouth did not move, but her words filled my mind.

Murderess. Murderess. Do you think you can hide from me, murderess? A life for a life.

Her words were like a sword stabbing into my heart.

Suddenly my mind was flooded with memories, unhappy memories of Paimu's hopeful face and my cruel last words to her. I could see and know how she felt. And even more than that, I felt her need for love and her awareness of her abandonment by the Algat. The utter rejection and hopelessness. All that time, I had the power to love, help, and comfort her.

But I had not done that. My sister had. I saw Nefret smiling down at her brown face and felt Paimu's joyful heart. The future became hopeful again. I then saw flashes of Paimu's memories—climbing the palm trees, plunging into the cool waters of the pool at Timia, playing with the baby goats, laughing with Alexio, stealing chula bread with Ziza. In the memories she shared, I could see Paimu's gap-toothed smile and feel the warmth within her. She who had been cast off had found love.

Then another memory.

I saw my own face in the darkness, rich robes around me, a queen's necklace hanging from my neck. Then the blade, and then the pain. I gasped at what I saw, yet I knew it was all true. I was the one who had done it.

I fell on my face and wept. The girl did not move. She did not offer comfort, nor did I expect it.

"What do you want? I cannot change what I have done. What do you want, Paimu? I am sorry I did this to you. I am sorry."

She moved closer. Still crying, I sat up on my knees and turned my face toward her. When I had the courage to open my eyes, I could see she was as she used to be. Her eyes were no longer black, her clothing was fresh, and her hair was brushed and clean. "What do you want?" I asked again. "I deserve to die. Take my life, Paimu. I surrender it to you." I meant what I said, but she did not accept my offer.

Then the dream changed. Paimu was not alone now. Farrah stood beside her, and together the three of us stood outside my tent at Timia. Farrah's hair fluttered up occasionally, lifted by a mysterious wind that blew around us. She did not rage at me, not as I had seen her do before on the other side of the temple walls, with eyes of hatred.

"Why have you come? To kill me?" I asked her. I was no longer kneeling but standing and wearing the robes of the mekhma. The cuts had disappeared from my flesh, although I could still feel the pain of them. Terror flooded me, and I wavered on my feet. A nearby fire lit up the darkness, and just beyond it, I could hear voices. Voices of many shadowy beings that watched my every move. There was nowhere to run. Nothing I could do.

"The price must be paid, Pah. The girl deserves justice."

"Are you asking me to take my own life? Is that what she wants?"

Farrah's expression was dark and unhappy, and she shook her head slowly.

"What is it, then? Tell me!"

"Kneel," she said.

Without question, I did as she told me. The girl stepped forward; she was mere inches from my face now. Tears slid down my face.

Let me die! I deserve this! This is justice!

I knew Paimu could hear my thoughts just as I had heard hers earlier. I thought about my sister, my father, and Alexio...

Ah, Alexio! I will miss you most of all!

Even as I thought those words, Paimu's hand reached out, and I felt an excruciating pain in my heart. I woke with a scream.

Magg shook me, babbling away in an attempt to silence me. I was sure if she'd had her way, she would have turned me out of her room, but I did not give her a choice. I fell into her arms, sobbing.

I knew what the girl wanted.

I knew I would have to give it to her.

Chapter Twelve

Golden Crown—Tadukhipa

"Come away, my love, and let me show you something," I leaned against the back of Amenhotep's neck, hoping he noticed and appreciated the feeling of my young breasts pressed against his flesh. He was hardly attentive, and as the weeks dragged by, it became more difficult to keep him entertained. He constantly pored over scrolls of reports, explored artifacts, and spent much of his time with the priests of the Aten. I frowned over his shoulder as he tinkered with the building model, moving pylons, obelisks and other architectural elements. I knew I had thus far failed in my missions—both of them.

When my father came to me, the tasks had seemed simple enough: seduce Amenhotep and show him the foolishness of abandoning the worship of Amun. How shortsighted of my husband to consider such a thing—the leopard coats had their hands in the workings of many nations. Their presence was growing in Mitanni, and with that growing presence came much wealth and prestige. There were other reasons, much more complex, but I had not paid much attention to these unimportant details. It was the challenge of seduction that delighted me. For the past two years, I could only observe Amenhotep, the son, from afar. But now that the old pharaoh was dead, I could finally turn my attention to more exciting things. Who wanted to make love to an old man? Thankfully, and many thanks to my concoctions, the father had not been able to raise his tent for me.

But I might as well have stayed in the Royal Harem for all the attention my new husband had given me. We had made love less than a handful of times during our time together. Although I made a great show to the servants of how tired I was each morning, these were pleasant lies. Even when he did come to me, he never stayed to sleep with me, nor did he linger long on my pillow after the deed was done.

I had secretly sent my dutiful little birds back to Thebes with messages that I prayed had gotten back to Nefertiti with all haste. I spread the "news" to the court that Amenhotep and I were closer than ever. Perhaps he had put his seed in my belly. Love and affection were not required for this.

Privately my magicians had told me that I *would* have a son, but I had yet to hold a baby in my arms.

So impatient, Tadukhipa, I could almost hear Inhapi scold me from the Otherworld.

I wondered how Nefertiti liked the gift I had sent her and if she was intelligent enough to understand it. With a smile, I imagined her expression when she realized that the brooch pin had been dipped in poison. I could see her skin grow paler as death claimed her. It had been a foolish thing to do, I knew, but I grew more desperate by the day. While I was here being ignored by my husband, she was ruling Egypt as his regent! It was more than I could bear, although I kept my thoughts to myself.

I rubbed his neck impatiently, but he did not turn from his models. "Soon," he said, reaching for his cup. With a sigh of exasperation, I left him alone and walked along the patio. This was a small palace, nothing as grand as the one in Thebes or the Royal Harem, and we had been here for a whole week. I grew bored with the scenery and his indifference. So far, I had not given voice to my disappointment. Better to smile and pretend how much I loved him. It was getting harder to do.

Aggravated, I reached for my robe and slid it over my nude body. I did not wish to show myself to the guards below, not that Amenhotep would mind. Still, I could not give up. I would not give up! To do so meant that the Desert Queen would win my place and I would lose the love and support of the Hittite throne.

Hadn't I paid enough? Hadn't I patiently endured the pawing of Amenhotep's father? I shivered, thinking of his dry, rough hands all over my body. Although he had not been man enough to take me, he had enjoyed pinching me and feeling my young flesh. I came to my new husband's bed a maid, technically. I did not think he even noticed when he pushed through the veil and made me bleed that first night. With a sigh, I pulled a flower off the vine that grew over the railing and toyed with it for a few minutes before I crushed it in my hand. I missed Inhapi. Her quick smile, her soft lips, her gentle fingers. What advice would she have given me right now?

"Amenhotep, come away now. It is getting late."

Eventually, he left his table and came to me. He wore no headdress today, no crown, but his height alone reminded me that he was Pharaoh. Kings were always taller than other men. My uncle, King of the Hittites, towered over his court, and Amenhotep was taller still. "What did you want to show me?"

"I have a surprise for you. It is in here," I said with my most flirtatious smile. He allowed me to lead him to the door of the inner chamber. The heady aroma of flowers filled the hallway, and just as I had instructed, baskets of blooms were everywhere. Somehow my servants had found night-blooming jasmine. The scent was said to stoke a man's desires. I turned my back to the door and stood between him and the handle. "Now, my king, on this last night here together, I have something special for you. Something you have never seen before."

He smiled patiently. "Something I have never seen before? My mind cannot fathom what it could be."

With a smile of satisfaction, I pushed the door open and ushered him into the chamber. The candlelight caught the golden mirrors on the walls and bounced around the room, making it seem like an enchanted place. Sitting on their knees in the middle of the bed were two young women with long golden hair. They wore nothing except shimmering belly chains and scented oils that gave their tanned skin a hint of gold. They looked like two delightful, magical creatures with their round curved hips and shapely arms and thighs. I sent them a stern look, reminding them to please my husband, then turned to Amenhotep with a seductive smile on my face.

"Have you ever seen such beauty before? And there are two of them. They are just for you, my king." Leaving him alone with his prizes, I walked out of the room and closed the door behind me. I waited a moment, listening to the young women giggling, and walked away happy that he did not refuse them.

So, he is not as pious and faithful as Nefertiti believes. That is something, at least.

I sauntered to my room. It was smaller than our shared chambers but elegantly decorated. I called my attendants and climbed into a bath to rest before tomorrow's journey. I did not see Amenhotep for the rest of the night, but it was no bother to me. I wanted to be alone so I could think of Inhapi without interruption. In a perfect world, we would still be together plotting our happy future. How I missed her!

I thought of Ramose and wondered if his bed was empty tonight. I'd once considered seducing the General of Egypt but had decided against it. I could not trust that he would be discreet. Ramose was a braggart, and he had loved Amenhotep the father. I wanted to feel close to my lost Inhapi, and what better way to do that than to lie with her husband? But I could not take that chance. Sitamen had disappointed me too. She pretended not to understand my invitations to experience the joys I could offer her. The girl spent all her time plucking away at threads, playing with her birds, and singing mournful songs. It was no matter. I had another distraction, for I would have a son—a son to rule—even if Amenhotep failed to give me one. I had to work quickly, for I feared that when I returned to Egypt, he would not call for me again. How would I explain away a child if too much time passed?

When I woke the following morning, I felt my stomach cramp. At first, I thought it was merely hunger, but the cramping got worse, and soon I felt blood trickling from between my legs. I reached down and looked at my hand. Yes, there it was—bright red blood. I was not pregnant. *Lying priests!* I turned into the pillow and screamed in frustration.

I was going to return to Thebes without a child in my womb. Nefertiti's belly would be swollen like a fat pear while I had nothing to show for my troubles. I heard my servants approaching my room and yelled at them. "Stay out. I will come out soon."

I could not let anyone know this. Not yet. How long before Amenhotep abandoned my bed forever? How that would please my enemy, Queen Tiye! How she would rock with laughter to hear that. Her son hated my bed and would never take me as his Great Wife! How delighted she would be when she learned the truth! I decided I must kill her. I thought the old witch would go down into the ground with her husband, but she did not. Too afraid to leave her son in my clutches.

Oh, Amenhotep! You infuriate me!

I knew that he pined for the Desert Queen—that he wanted to make her the Great Wife. I knew he wanted her more than he had ever wanted me. The only thing stopping him from announcing it from the top of the palace were the Hittites, my family. The same family who abandoned me to the whims of Egypt's kings long ago. Amenhotep already believed I carried his child. I had been two months without a flow, I all but declared it. I could not face his disappointment now.

No. I would have to find another way. I would have a child, and I knew who could help me. As I cleaned up the blood and rinsed my stained nightgown, I quickly fomented a plan.

I was not defeated yet.

Chapter Thirteen

The Burning Bull—Ramose

I desired Sitamen like I had never desired another woman. At the beginning of my marriage, Inhapi had stirred my sense of dignity and duty with her cool seductive looks. With her, I was the General of Egypt, an unappreciated noble waiting to be recognized for my brilliance and strength. With Ayn, I was the rescuer, the strange and distant man who brought pleasure without any demands. There had been others, but they had been meaningless meetings. The grappling of flesh. Needed release. Like eating a meal or drinking a tasty wine. These had been nothing more than wasted moments.

But with Sitamen, I could be Ramose. She neither showered me with flowery speech nor treated me like a stud horse. I did not take her as some women liked a man to do. We embraced one another like people, and for the first time, I knew what the poets were talking about with their verses of stars and fate. How was it that a few weeks could seem like a happy eternity? How could it feel as if this had been the only true reality for me?

I felt loved, and I knew I did not deserve it.

I nodded stupidly as Aperel told me about the training for the new horses. I thought of Sitamen's silky hair falling in her eyes as she smiled at me, one shoulder bare and vulnerable. Kafta and I drilled with swords as I oversaw the training of my neglected soldiers. He struck me with the wooden blade and laughed at me. "Head in the clouds, General?" Kafta knew my secret, but I trusted him. I did not answer him—how could I deny it? Even as I bobbed my head to avoid his strike, deep beneath the arc of his practice blade, I could see her walking peacefully among her caged birds like a strange bird goddess. Seeing her with Kames made me love her more. It was as if she were the boy's mother. It was a happy fantasy. A fantasy that would surely change now that Pharaoh was returning to Thebes. Too many people already knew about our meetings. No matter how carefully we arranged our time together, we could not avoid the gossiping tongues forever. Every day I told myself that I must end this, but every evening I fell asleep in Sitamen's arms happy and satisfied.

Tonight, out of an abundance of caution, I waited until dark and walked into the palace using the commoners' entrance near the cooking houses. My stomach rumbled at the smells of baking bread, roasted meat, and garlic. A familiar guard acknowledged me but wisely kept his mouth shut. I walked quickly to Sitamen's private chambers, avoiding as many people as I could. It was difficult to do in a palace where hundreds were employed tending to a member of the royal family.

"Look, Kames! Here is your father!" I smiled at Sitamen, who held my son as I laid my sword and belt on a nearby table. She liked me to remove them before I held the child. "See how strong he is, little one? You will be just like your father one day." She kissed the baby's cheek and then stood on her tiptoes and kissed mine.

My arms slid around her waist, and I hugged her to me. With a quick kiss, I accepted the peaceful bundle she offered me and rubbed the child's chin with my rough finger. He opened his eyes and stared at me as if he had something to say. "Fine boy. He grows heavier every day." I never knew what to say to him, but I liked holding him in my arms. "Have you kept the princess busy today?"

She laughed, and it was a pleasant sound. "Indeed, he did not. He slept all day, but he watched the birds in between naps." She poured wine into two cups, and we talked for a while before one of her servants took the child away to do whatever it was that small children did. I watched him disappear.

Sitamen's servant raced into the room unannounced and wide-eyed. "Lady! Your mother is here! I could not stop her."

Just then, the Queen walked into our chambers, her pink robes swinging about her tiny frame. I had forgotten how small she was, how absolutely frail she had become since Amenhotep's journey to the Otherworld. She regarded me coolly. "So, it is true. I never thought you to be a fool, General."

"Queen Tiye!" I rose to my feet but quickly remembered this was my late Pharaoh's wife. I did not think it wise to answer her beyond that, so I kept my peace.

Sitamen's eyes were riveted on her mother as the older woman turned her attention to her. "And you. Your brother will undoubtedly know about this. If I know, he knows! Do you know what this means for you? You will *never* be the wife of Pharaoh now. Any chance you had is gone, along with your reputation. You have broken the law, Sitamen, and you have condemned this man to death." Tiye's pale hand waved toward me, and her voice had an honest edge of fear to it. "Have you learned nothing from me, foolish girl?"

Sitamen threw her cup on the floor, and the wine splashed up and stained the hem of her mother's garments. "Oh, I would say that I have learned plenty from you, Queen Tiye! I have learned that if I do not find my own happiness, I will never have it."

"Happiness? Who told you happiness was afforded to you? You are Pharaoh's daughter—and wife! No one cares about your happiness."

"I know this lesson. I learned it at an early age." Sitamen slid her arm through mine and held me tightly. I cupped her hand with mine. I had to do something, say something.

"Queen Tiye, I love Sitamen. I never meant for this to happen, but I am willing to pay whatever price I must."

Sitamen said softly, "Ramose! I will talk to my brother. He will understand."

The old queen snorted. "Even if he does, there is nothing he can do to help you, Sitamen. If he finds you together like this, if someone brings him ample evidence, you might as well cut your own throat. He will obey the law, I promise you. How could you betray us like this, General? My husband loved you like a son. He trusted you with his kingdom, and now you bring his daughter to ruin."

"How dare you speak to him like that, as if he betrayed my father? All he has done is love me. Is that a crime?"

"In fact, it is a crime, Sitamen!"

"How dare you speak so sanctimoniously when everyone knows that you and my uncle…" Tiye crossed the short distance between us in a flash and struck Sitamen's face with her open hand. Sitamen pulled her hand away from me and gasped in surprise.

"You have been listening to Tadukhipa, haven't you, evil girl? How can you believe such lies?"

"Why are you here, Mother? To gloat? To condemn me, or better still, throw me into the fire yourself?" Sitamen did not cry or hunker down. She touched the red handprint on her face briefly, and then with clenched fists, stood still.

Queen Tiye's hawkish eyes were on me now. "If I were you, I would think of your son."

"What do you mean?"

"Don't listen to her, Ramose. My brother would never harm Kames, and I have claimed him as my own. Remember?"

I wanted to believe Sitamen's words, but I had seen firsthand the ruthlessness of kings. At Pharaoh's command, I had executed men for much less than my own crimes. "What do you advise?" I asked Queen Tiye.

"Ramose?" Sitamen stood between us, facing me now. The look on her face was a turbulent mixture of disappointment and disbelief.

"I love you, Sitamen. I have never said that to another woman, not even Inhapi, but we must think of Kames. I know you love him as I do."

"Do not listen to her. Nobody knows about us. If you listen, she will destroy us."

I could see there would be no reasoning with her. Tiye was right. If she knew about Sitamen and me, then Amenhotep would surely know too. Seeking her help might be the only way my son could survive. I asked again, "What would you have me do, Queen Tiye?"

"Throw yourself at my son's feet and tell him that Sitamen seduced you. That she compelled you—no, commanded you—to stay with her."

"That is not true!" Sitamen shouted.

"Do you want to save this man or not? If you do not shoulder some of the blame, he is doomed. Do you know the punishment for this? They will cast him into the flames to purify him, Sitamen. He will burn as the law demands."

"I do not believe you! Amenhotep—"

"Will do what the priests tell him." In a softer voice, she said, "You should listen to me, Ramose. It is the only way. There will be nowhere to hide for you."

"I cannot allow Sitamen to take the blame. She is innocent."

Queen Tiye drew herself up and sighed. "I leave that to you. At least in this, you are an honorable man."

Sitamen wailed. "I cannot allow you to do this. I won't, Ramose. All will be well. I know it!" She laid her head on my chest, and I held her, uncaring that Tiye witnessed the demonstration of my affection. I kissed the top of her head, and we said nothing for a long minute.

"You have to go. Leave Kames with me. I promise you no harm will come to him. Amenhotep would never injure a child. Go now and let me reason with him."

"I cannot run away. All Egypt knows who I am, and I will not let the weight of this fall on you. Let me go to him. I will do as your mother suggests, and let us see how things go."

"No. Don't leave, Ramose." She sobbed and clung to me with all her might.

"Take care of Kames, Sitamen. Promise me." Through moist eyes and wet cheeks, she agreed begrudgingly. I grasped her arms and pushed her away.

"No! Ramose!"

Her sobs rang in my ears as I walked down the corridor, my heart pounding with fear. Not for myself but for Kames and Sitamen. I knew what my punishment would be.

Queen Tiye spoke the truth.

There would be no mercy. I would burn.

Chapter Fourteen

Moment of Forgetting—Tiye

Sitamen screamed at me, "How can you do this? Why did you come here?"

"I did not create this disastrous situation. You did. And by doing so, you left us open to attack from the Hittite woman and all our enemies! Don't you know that even now the kingdom hangs in the balance? Your brother is new to his throne and weak in the eyes of the world."

She wiped her nose with her hand. Her hair came unbound and hung around her face in tangles, catching the excess moisture on her cheeks. It clung to her most unattractively. She tucked the hair behind her large ears and continued to yell at me. "What enemies? Which ones? Do you think I don't know what this is about? This is about you and Kiya! Will this feud never end? Now you have taken everything from me, Mother. Everything!"

No matter how hard I tried to keep my heart a stone, I could not help but feel sympathy for her. She was like a leaf in a bowl of water on a windy day. She always had been. Turning this way and that with no focus, no dream that was real. Sitamen had suffered the disease many spoiled princesses suffered. Daydreaming. I had warned her to turn her attention to real life, but she had not heeded my words. "No matter what you think, Sitamen, I never wanted to come here. I saw this in the water. I did not come right away because I wanted you to have more time. I hoped it was a false vision. But when even Huya heard the gossip, I had to come and see for myself. It was either your brother or me. Which do you prefer?" When she did not answer me, I continued, "Why do you think I always kept you at arm's length, daughter?"

"Now you call me daughter?"

Ignoring her disrespect, I continued, "Because I knew you would have this life—a life with no husband, no lover, no children—and I could not stand to watch it unfold. I should have known you would do something like this!"

"Like what? Love a man? Love Ramose? Want a child of my own? Desire the things all women have?"

"Women never choose their own destinies."

"But you did, didn't you, *Mother*? You were not the daughter of Pharaoh, yet here you stand. The Great Wife of my father, Amenhotep. You have always done as you chose, and you always chose what was best for you."

"What do you mean?"

"You did not mishear me. As always, you think of yourself above anyone. I wish to the gods you were not my mother. I wish anyone were my mother except you!"

I grabbed her arms and held her tight, even though she twisted and tried to pull away from me.

"Let me go! I want to die!"

Many young women said foolish things when love disappointed them, but something in Sitamen's voice told me I should believe her. I had seen her in the water, her face the picture of anguish. She reached toward the flames and screamed, "Ramose!" I saw my son with a cold look in his eyes, watching as the man burned for his crimes against Pharaoh. And I saw one more thing. I could not let it happen! I could not! I would stay with her whether she said yea or nay. Until there was officially a new Great Queen, I held that role.

"I will not let you go, Sitamen. You cannot leave me, and I will not leave you. Perhaps I have not been the best mother to you, but I am here now. And I swear to you, I will not leave you."

Sitamen fell onto her bed of blue silk and curled into a ball. I sat in an uncomfortable chair and watched her cry. I did not touch her or disturb her in her grief. She loved Ramose, I had no doubt. Perhaps he loved her too, but it was of little matter now. Huya would have found him and led him to Pharaoh's palace to await Pharaoh's decision. It would be out of our hands. Better that I tell him than Tadukhipa or some other. When I could, I would plead for the man, but I knew how it would go for him. The law could not be undone. It had never been undone. To lie with the daughter or wife of Pharaoh meant death. Doubly so if she was both. There would be nothing for Ramose but fire in the belly of the bull. I shuddered, thinking about the massive golden bull. The priests of Amun would prepare it, making it shine like the sun before they stuffed Ramose inside it and lit the flames. It was a horrible thing to witness.

Once, a wife and half-sister of my husband had done the same thing—slept with another man. Amenhotep was fond of her, but it did not matter. The law remained the law. She burned in the belly of the bull along with her lover. It had been so long ago that I could not remember either of their names, but it had been a cruel thing indeed. "Why not give them poison to drink or remove their heads?" I had asked my husband.

His words were, "The law is the law."

And that was the way it was. No amount of tears or love would change that. Not for anyone, even young Sitamen.

Time passed. I grew hungry, but I remained in the chair even when the servants came into the room to raise the curtains and light the torches. One young servant brought in a tray of food to tempt Sitamen to eat. She stared at the girl as if she did not hear her, but I knew she did. Instead, she rolled over and gazed at the moon. It rose perfectly round in the purple sky, and the stars shone happily, completely unaware of the evil that would soon befall the great General of Egypt and possibly his young lover. What would her father say? What would he do if he were here?

Someone brought the baby into the room. He cried a little, but Sitamen did not show any interest in him. I asked the wet nurse, "What is his name again? I forgot."

"Kames, Great Queen. He is the son of..."

"I know whose son he is. He is my grandson and the son of my daughter, Sitamen. She has adopted him as her own."

Sitamen sat up in her bed, and for the first time today I saw a glimmer of happiness on her face. She reached for Kames, and I gave him to her. "Thank you, Great Queen," she whispered sadly.

I nodded and stepped back. My words made it law. Let any man—even my son—say differently. He could not! I stared down at the baby. He was a handsome child with dark-fringed lashes, warm, light brown skin, and a nose like his father's. I saw nothing of the foreign girl in him. He would be the image of his father, of that I had no doubt. Well, if Sitamen could not have the father, at least she would have the son. This I could do for her. If she lived.

"Excuse me, Great Queen, your son is here to see you and Queen Sitamen." Huya's eyes told me everything I needed to know. He avoided making eye contact. His bow was stiff and formal. This was not a random visit. Pharaoh had indeed heard the rumors, or had perhaps heard it from the General's own lips.

Now we would see where the fates fell. I made the sign against curses behind my back in case Tadukhipa was behind this. I would not put it past her to curse us all.

I did not mock Amenhotep by pretending I did not know the reason for his sudden visit. He stormed into the room, fists clenched. He paused at the foot of Sitamen's bed and stared down at her and the child.

"Is this your child, Sitamen? Is this Ramose's child? Confess what you have done! He has already told me from his own lips that he has lain with you. He believes he is in love with you. I had him beaten!"

Amenhotep tore off the cover, and I took the baby from Sitamen, afraid my son would strike her. I had never seen him so angry.

"I adopted Ramose's child. Kames is not my blood, but he has my name. Mother spoke it."

He turned his head to me, his blue- and gold-striped headpiece swinging sharply, and his eyes flashed with anger. "You did this?"

"The father will die, won't he? Allow the son to live. He is only a baby, not guilty of anything except being born to Ramose. I've declared it so already. And..." I continued cautiously, "I am still Great Queen unless you have chosen a wife to take my place. If you have not, it is my right."

"Your right? You approve of this? Did you know the whole time? My own General! Lying with my sister under my very nose! Sitamen! Why?"

"Because you would never have me, and you cannot give me to anyone else. I had no choice. I love him, Amenhotep! I love Ramose! He has my heart, and I have his! Please have mercy! He has been a faithful servant to you. Please, brother! You have always been so kind and good to me. Please. I will never ask you for another thing!"

"Indeed, you will not. Ramose is going to burn as soon as the Aten rises. I cannot stop it, for the priests of Amun are even now polishing their bull and readying it for the sacrifice. And as for you, I command you to be in attendance. You will watch what you have done to the man you say you love."

"No, please, Amenhotep. Do not do this! I cannot believe you would kill your friend and the man I love! Look upon the son I have adopted—Ramose's son! Please!"

"You make it worse each time you say his name! Speak no more to me, Sitamen. I am Pharaoh Amenhotep, and I command that Sitamen, my wife and sister, shall no more speak to me. If she does, she will also die in the fire!"

I shouted, "Son! You cannot do this! You cannot condemn your sister like this! Have mercy on her! She is your blood and flesh. You are both the fruit of my womb! Amenhotep, listen to me!"

"No more, Great Queen! No more words on this subject." I could see that he was crying, nearly sobbing himself. "Why? Why did they do this? We could have found another way, but now I cannot change it. Ramose will burn in the bull, and Sitamen will witness it. Where is the child?"

I took the baby in my arms and refused to hand him over. So angry was my son that I could not trust him. I would never have imagined this day would ever come.

"I command you as your Pharaoh to give me the child, Mother."

Hesitatingly, I did as he asked. I prayed to the Aten to protect Kames, and I made sure Amenhotep heard me doing so.

He held him as Sitamen writhed pitifully in her bed, sobbing from the depths of her soul. One of the physicians had arrived during our discourse and was now forcing the girl to drink a dose of calming medicine. In just a few seconds I could see it take effect. She became very still, her voice quiet and calm. She had that dreamy look in her eyes as she watched everything. Pharaoh walked around the room with the baby in his arms. Possibly sensing the danger and the anger of the king, the baby began to wail and cry. Amenhotep walked to the balcony and then stopped. For one terror-filled moment, I imagined the worst.

I pleaded, "No, Amenhotep. Imagine your own son, protected and safe in his mother's belly. What has this child had? No mother, now no father. Please do not harm him. Give him to me, and you will never have to see him again. I will care for him. I swear you will never see or hear from him again."

Considering my words for a moment, he extended his arms to me and gave me the baby. "As if I would have harmed him," he said in a rough voice. "See to it that you keep your word, Mother."

As quickly as I could, I left the room with the child, but I was gone only long enough to return him to his wet nurse. I raced back to Sitamen's room. Sitting on the edge of her bed and staring down at her was Amenhotep. She stared back with a blank expression.

"If she had come to me, we might have found a way. I can do nothing now."

"Sitamen loves Ramose. I am sure of it."

"And unfortunately for her, her love comes with a death sentence. I mourn for him. In a different world, I would have welcomed him as a brother-in-law, but it cannot be. We have the Phares blood, and it cannot be mingled with any other kind."

I wanted to say, *What about your father? He married me, didn't he?* However, I kept my peace.

"So, death is the only option?" I sat on the other side of the bed. I knew Sitamen could hear us, but she would not remember our words or understand them.

"You know this."

"I do."

"I saw her in the water, my son. I saw her dying. I cannot let her die. I have been a poor mother to her, but I refuse to let her die! I will stay with her every moment of the day to prevent it."

"Yes, stay with her, Mother. Keep her safe. I must go now."

"Go see your queen, Amenhotep, and forget this for the night. I will see you tomorrow."

With a nod of agreement, he left me, casting one last sad look at his sister, who stared into the sky and drooled, the medicine taking full effect. I would have to talk to the physician and ask for more, or she would never survive the burning of Ramose in the morning.

How could this have happened? My poor, sweet daughter.

Then I remembered something I heard a long time ago. Amenhotep and I had visited the Three Oracles at Majayat on our honeymoon. Those old witches were ancient then, and surely they were dead now. We had entered their cave, our hands full of the pearls they loved. We left our gifts at their feet, and they told us what we wanted to know. We would have many children, but many would die. All those who died could have lived, but because of our stars, we had doomed them all to live unfulfilled lives. First, Thutmose died, then his little brother. So small and unformed was he that I did not name him. Now the prophecy of the Oracles reached out across time to claim Sitamen too. I would not allow this!

As she began to fall asleep, I slid in the bed beside her. The baby was gone now with the nervous nursemaid, who promised to never leave Kames alone. I lay beside Sitamen and pulled her slack body to mine. It was easy to do, for she was small too. I stroked her hair and touched her face just as I used to do when she was a child.

My daughter! Amenhotep's daughter! How cruel I have been to you! How I love you, daughter!

I fell asleep with tears on my skin. I thought I had lost the ability to cry, but I was wrong. Tears had been there all along.

I needed them tonight. As the servants snuffed out the lights, I began to pray quietly to Isis. If she did not intervene and prevent this disaster, I would worship her no more. I told her so, but I heard nothing in return.

With a last sigh, I fell asleep and did not dream.

Chapter Fifteen

Children of the Aten—Nefertiti

I stormed through the gates of the temple, passing the first pylon without much notice. A row of gigantic statues faced me. The statue of Queen Tiye wore a short, round wig, and her stone husband sat stiffly beside her. Frozen in a moment of time, the couple appeared happy to receive guests at Amun's temple. I was sure she felt differently about it now. After all, these priests had murdered my husband's brother and plundered the fortunes of Egypt without fear. Nobody protested much, but everyone knew the truth. By killing the older brother, they had unintentionally driven my husband to worship the Aten. In doing so, he abandoned centuries of tradition, and that was not an easy thing for the leopard coats to stomach.

Later today, I would see my husband for the first time in months. I knew he was back in Thebes, although he had not come to me last night. I had a growing sense of fear that he had chosen Tadukhipa over me, but I had one last task to do. One more thing to accomplish before I relinquished my role as regent.

Today I wore a long, flowing red robe to show my anger. Let them interpret that as anger for Ramose—the news of that scandal had rocked the capital—but it was truly the priests of Amun who stirred my rage. I pulled my red hair back tightly to hide it and wore a dark wig with no adornment. I was going to see this golden beast, the place where they often burned children to their god. It was an abomination to my eyes and to the parents of those who were sacrificed. What kind of god would allow such things to be done in his or her name? It would stop today!

Menmet had told me about the sacrifice that was scheduled for this morning. Heby had whispered the secret in her ear, and she told me swiftly, loyal servant that she was. I forbade her from coming with me. I did not want Heby to be angry with her, but I was sure he would eventually find out the truth.

I had never been to the temple of Amun. Never had I laid a sacrifice at the feet of the god there, and never would I. Not since I learned of their despicable practices, practices that Amenhotep would learn about. I passed the second pylon and barely glanced at the four statues that faced me. I did not know their names, but I made the sign of respect to them. My servants looked puzzled, but I did not need to explain anything to them. I kept walking. An unfamiliar leopard coat came toward me. He looked amused at my approach.

"Queen Nefertiti," he called as if he were calling an old friend. I did not pause but kept walking. "Wait, my queen! We are not accustomed to royal guests entering the temple without prior notice. What can we help you with?"

Still not speaking to the leopard-coated evil one, I gave my guard, Kemaza, a hard stare. The guard stepped between the priest and me, forbidding him to speak to me again.

I said, "Come now, Harwa. Let us see the truth of the matter."

"Down here, Queen Nefertiti." Harwa pointed to a low staircase. I paused at the top of the stairs, seeing only darkness. I was angry, but my mind also suspected treachery. Treachery abounded in Egypt. That much was true. The place drew evil into it like a spider summoned flies and insects. Just like Astora. She had been evil, but I would never know now what had compelled her to come here. Omel had done his best to show me he knew nothing of her intentions, but I did not believe him. Harwa, though? He had given me no reason not to trust him, and he had been recommended by the old queen. I trusted her above everyone else here.

"I will go first, my queen."

"No, I will go." I glided down the stairs quickly and heard the shocked voices of the priests. I walked amongst them, looking each in the eye. Maya stood watching, a blade in his hand. A child cowered at his feet. It was as I had heard, then. They were sacrificing children here.

"You will put down that knife and leave that child alone, Maya!"

He was so angry at my intrusion that he appeared ready to spit on me or stab me, perhaps both. I did not cower. "You think to interrupt the god's worship? You do not command me, Desert Queen! You have no authority here! Get out now and leave with your life, if you value it!"

"You have distorted the worship of Amun! This is not true worship! No god of Egypt has ever asked for the life of a child, yet you kill them with your own hands."

"These children were given to the god, and we use them as we see fit. Now leave, or I won't tell you again."

I reached for the half-naked little boy. He had a fearful look on his dirty, pinched face.

"Come to me, little one!" I said as the priest approached me. The other priests stepped toward me too, but my guards were ready to shove their spears into anyone who withstood me. The boy clung to my leg, and the other children ran to me. There must have been at least thirty here in this dank, dirty cellar. The massive stone bowl in the center was on fire, but I could see that none had been burned yet today. Such hopelessness in the faces of the children. I wanted to pick them all up. Instead, I clapped my left hand over my stomach and took the child by the hand with my right.

The priest grinned at me threateningly and stared at my belly. "Try it," I said to him in a venomous whisper.

"Please, if my queen fancies a few children, take them. There will be more tomorrow. You cannot stop the worship, my queen."

"Hear me now, priests." I spun in a circle. "I claim all these children for the Aten. They belong to him now! These, and those that come after them!" The priests hissed at me, but I continued, "These are the Children of the Aten! You will cease your unholy worship this day. No more will you spill the blood of a child here. My guards will be here every day to make sure you obey my command."

"You cannot do this," Maya screamed at me, his anger reaching a dangerous level.

"I can, and I have."

"I curse you, Queen Nefertiti. You will never carry that child to term. He will die in his mother's womb, drowning in his own blood!"

I gasped and raised my arm as if I could protect myself from his curse with it. Then I heard a shout from behind me. "Not before I kill you!"

Amenhotep!

His words echoed through the smelly room like a saving wind. I turned to him as a smile spread across my face. "My husband and Pharaoh, I have claimed these children for the Aten. Let them come serve the true god of light and love. I cannot sit idly by while these innocents give their lives for these greedy priests."

"And so it shall be done. All children given to Amun are now the property of the Aten. They are indeed Children of the Aten. Is there anyone who would argue with me?"

No one spoke a word against him, although it seemed like he hoped they would. Only Maya continued to look unafraid, challenging him still.

"And for what you have said to my wife, the Great Wife of Amenhotep, you shall pay. Seize him now!"

The guards rushed to do my husband's bidding, and together we went up the stairs with the children. Many were lame and had to have help walking. A few priests, those who were intelligent enough to know which way the wind was blowing, decided to help us in our task. In fact, at least five removed their leopard skins, happy that someone had stopped the evil practice. They bowed low before us and begged us to allow them to help.

The children were hungry, confused, and convinced they were going to die. I held on to the boy and let him cling to my leg without refusing him. Amenhotep gathered me in his arms. "How did you know I was here?" I asked him.

"I am Pharaoh. Do you think I do not know what you do, my love?"

"My love. How I love to hear you say that! Let us take the children to the Aten temple. I have already spoken to the priests there. They have a place prepared for the children. They will treat them with respect and teach them the ways of the Aten. Soon, your whole kingdom will worship him."

"You never cease to amaze me, my wife."

The children were carried away, and we walked outdoors to make the journey to our palace. Many people had gathered to clap and cheer for us. They heard what we were doing and were grateful for our help. Parents who had lost their children as debts to the temple received them back. Children who were unwanted or had nowhere to go were invited to stay at the Aten's temple. It was a truly revolutionary day.

"You did not hear me, did you?"

"What do you mean?"

"You are now the Great Wife. My only wife and my love."

I could hardly believe what I was hearing. "I thought the Hittites... The trials... What about..."

"You let me worry about those things. You just keep doing what you are doing. All will be well. Harwa and my mother have told me everything. You have done well, Nefertiti. You are Egypt's true queen, but celebration must wait." His face changed completely.

I could see the subject pained him, but I asked anyway. "What has happened, my love? What worries you so?"

"You have heard, I am sure. Ramose was found with my sister. He will be burned this morning in the Golden Bull—the one in the temple courtyard here—and there is nothing I can do. It is the law. In fact, I go there now. I do not expect you to witness this. Go home, and I will meet you there."

"No," I said. "My place is at your side. I must be there for Sitamen too."

"You should know that I have forbidden her to speak to me. And when the burning is complete, she will be banished from here."

"No, Amenhotep! Say it is not true. She is your sister!"

"It is the law, Nefertiti. There is nothing I can do."

"Yes, there is. Just like we stopped the sacrifice, we can do this too."

Then I saw the truth. Amenhotep did not want to save Ramose or Sitamen. It surprised me, and for the first time, I saw my husband in a new light. He was not perfect as I imagined but flawed, jealous, and easy to provoke in areas of loyalty and respect.

"But she has adopted his son. I had hoped to send him away too, but my mother interceded on his behalf. That should please you since you love children so," he said, looking at me steadily.

We stepped out of the dark rooms and climbed up yet another level to the auditorium that overlooked the Golden Bull. The fire under it had been built. Occasionally, a priest would toss a living thing, like a rabbit or a snake, into the fire to test the heat. Whatever they consigned to the flames died quickly. I hoped it would be the same for Ramose. He had not been my friend, but he had brought the Meshwesh home to Zerzura. And Ayn had loved him. *Ayn! I am so glad you cannot see this!* The place began to fill up with witnesses called to see justice done.

Queen Tiye stood by her daughter, Sitamen. The girl looked sick, as if at any minute she would throw up on her mother, but Tiye did not leave her side. I could see the worry in the old queen's face.

Others came too. I saw members of the court, including the scribes, Memre, Huya, and so many familiar faces. Even Tadukhipa made an appearance. She wore all her elegance, which seemed out of place since she was about to witness the death of her friend Inhapi's husband. It did not appear to matter to her.

Surprisingly there was not much pomp in the proceedings. Ramose was brought out, and Sitamen's cries grew louder and more pitiful. She called his name. He looked up at her and smiled as if to say, "All is well."

Standing so close to Pharaoh, I could see the tears in his eyes as he said, "Ramose, General of Egypt. You have been found guilty of adultery with Sitamen, my sister and wife. Therefore, you are consigned to the flames to burn. But since you have been my friend and a friend to my father, I do not deny you access to the Otherworld. You will be buried in a grave that is befitting your station, and all manner of things will be done to facilitate your journey to my father's side. While you leave in shame, you will arrive in peace. Serve him in the Otherworld as you served him here."

"What of my son, Pharaoh? Please. What of my son?"

Suddenly I spoke up. I had not planned to speak, but I did. "I, Nefertiti, am now the Great Wife of Amenhotep. As my first act, I claim your son as my own, as our own. He will be raised in our household and eat at our table."

Tiye and Amenhotep shot me a look of surprise, but neither said anything. Tadukhipa's face crumpled, and she steadied herself by putting her hand out to the servant who stood next to her.

"Thank you, Great Queen, Nefertiti. It is more than I deserve."

I nodded at Ramose and ignored Amenhotep's shocked expression. I watched sadly as the handsome, brave general of Egypt was bound with ropes and stripped of his clothing. He would leave this world as he entered it.

"No! No, Ramose! Please, let me go, Mother! Ramose!" Sitamen pulled and tugged, but Tiye would not let her go.

Four large priests stood beside the golden bull. They whispered something to the doomed man and held out a cup, probably offering him a drug to help him cope with the flames. He obediently took a few sips, then looked up and said, "I love you, Sitamen. Forgive me, Pharaoh, but I do, although this is a great sin. I pray that this fire will purge me."

"Amenhotep," I whispered in desperation. Even as I said it, I knew I could not stop this—and neither could he. The priests came and picked up Ramose. Without much warning, they pitched him into the fire, and he began to writhe and scream. Suddenly, a flock of birds flew over the fiery bowl, circling it as if they were there to witness the death of the brave man. Ramose screamed as the priests stoked the fire higher. He would die soon, but the agony he would suffer, no one would ever forget.

Sitamen quit her struggling. She seemed transfixed by the birds that swirled above Ramose. They were unusual birds, bluebirds, and not the kind that normally liked to scavenge a burning body—or any body, for that matter. As her attendants pointed at the unusual sight, one of them let loose of her hand. I saw her face. I knew what she would do, but before I could speak, Sitamen ran with all her might and leaped over the rail, her arms outstretched as if she too could fly. Instead, she tumbled into the fiery pit below. She joined Ramose in the fire, and together they screamed until they were dead. The guards ran to rescue her, but the heat was so great that no one could have gotten near the pit without losing their own life.

Then Tiye let out a cry of agony, summoning it from the depths of her soul. "Sit-a-men! My daughter!"

Amenhotep was on his feet reaching for her, but it did not matter. He raced down the stairs to stop the proceedings, but it was too late. They were dead, bound together for all eternity.

Amenhotep cried out and cursed Amun. "I will never serve you, murdering god! Do you hear me? Never!" He stormed out of the temple, and I walked behind him. We would never set foot in another temple of Amun as long as we lived.

The news of the deaths of Ramose and Sitamen had not yet reached the populace, for they greeted us with joyful cries. Amenhotep pulled the litter closed and wept with all his heart. I sat beside him and held him close. What could I say? Nothing. His misery was complete.

Too soon the litter stopped. We stepped out, knowing that we would face the crowd again. While they did not yet know that Ramose was dead, that Sitamen had sacrificed herself for love, they did know that I was now the Queen of Egypt, the Great Wife of Amenhotep.

"Hail, Great Wife!" they cheered. Amenhotep put on a smile. He was not happy or in the mood to celebrate, but we could not deny the people their moment. Sadness would come soon enough.

"Hail to you, people of Egypt."

One of my servants appeared with bags of coins. Amenhotep directed me to cast the coins to the people, and so I did. I showered gold upon them, and they cheered me as if I were Isis herself. As I did, I spotted a face in the crowd, a face I had not expected to see. It was the face of my sister, Pah. I looked again, and she was gone.

Then I heard some words, her words, as if they were whispered in my ear, "Hafa-nu, mekhma Nefret. Hafa-nu!"

"Hafa-nu!" I cried loudly to the people. They did not hesitate to call back using the Meshwesh blessing. Soon all of the people gathered, most of the people of Thebes, were speaking the words of the Red Lands, "Hafa-nu!"

Amenhotep stood beside me and whispered in my ear, "You have done what I asked. The people love you, Nefertiti. This is truly your kingdom, and I am your slave."

I kissed him. I probably should not have done so, not after all we had seen that morning and all the heartache that was still to come, but I kissed him. The crowd cheered again, and I reveled in the moment. Even then I knew there would be few moments like this one.

As baskets of flowers were poured out upon us, we stood together for that glorious moment and let the people celebrate. Whether they realized it or not, we were in a new age, an age of peace and love. Let this morning's sacrifice be the last. I was more determined than ever to let love reign in Thebes and in all the Red and Black Lands.

I could do it. I could make it happen.

This was my kingdom, and I was finally Nefertiti.

Read on for an excerpt from the final chapter of the Desert Queen saga:

The Song of the Bee-Eater

Queen Tiye dawdled into my chamber this morning before my bath, her face askew with worry. "Where have you hidden the baby, Desert Queen? Where is Kames? Give me Kames."

I pulled the robe back on and came to her. I held her bony hand in mine and patted it. "He is a baby no longer, Great Queen. He is a man now and in Pharaoh's service. He has gone on a diplomatic trip to the west. You will see him soon."

I led her to a nearby padded couch. I couldn't believe she'd arrived unattended and in the shape she was in. She wore no wig, and her natural hair, thin and curly, sprang up around her face like an unruly cloud. She'd slept in her makeup—slick streaks of kohl slid down the side of her face, and her lips were ringed with stiff red paint.

"Oh, yes, I remember now. What of Thutmose? Has he come home yet?" She spoke now of her own son, dead at least twenty-five years.

I could not break her heart again this morning, so I told her a pleasant lie instead. I knew the pain of losing a child. I had lost three myself, and the grief never left me. "No, Great Queen. He is still away, but he too will return soon. For now, it is just you and me." I squeezed her hand and poured her a cup of water, which she accepted.

Her hands shook, but she drank the water until the cup was empty. Setting it on the table, she took in the view of the room. "I like this room. I've always liked this room. It feels very cool in here, and there are no bats. I dislike bats."

"Yes, it is very cool here. And I never see bats. Are you hungry, Queen Tiye?"

"No, I am not." She rubbed at her nose with her finger and eyed me. "My son is very lucky to have you, Nefertiti."

What to say to that? If she were whole and hale, I'd beg her for help. I'd throw myself at her feet and plead with her to speak to her son for me. But she was not. This was only a fragile shell of the intelligent, quick-witted, sometimes cruel woman I knew. And as far as I knew, Akhenaten no longer allowed her in his court. We were like two cast-off queens, forgotten and wished dead. Such a sad ending, but it wasn't really the end, was it? Pah's words from last night rang in my mind, and I had tried all morning to pretend none of it had happened. How could I leave the people I loved behind? Tiye needed me. It was she who had brought me here. She'd been the very Hand of Destiny that led the Falcon of the Red Lands to the throne of Egypt. Now she was losing her mind and had no one to care for her. When Huya was living he took great pains to hide her condition, but now that the old man was gone, there was no one else. No one she would trust. Except me.

Connect with M.L. Bullock on Facebook[1]. To receive updates on her latest releases, visit her website at M.L. Bullock[2] and subscribe to her mailing list. You can also contact her at authormlbullock@gmail.com.

About the Author

Author of the best-selling *Seven Sisters* series and the *Gulf Coast Paranormal* series, M.L. Bullock has been storytelling since she was a child. A student of archaeology, she loves weaving stories that feature her favorite historical characters—including Nefertiti. She currently lives on the Gulf Coast with her family but travels frequently to explore the southern states she loves so much.

1.   https://www.facebook.com/AuthorMLBullock

2.   http://www.mlbullock.com

Also by M.L. Bullock

Desert Queen Saga
The Tale of Nefret
The Falcon Rises
The Kingdom of Nefertiti
The Song of the Bee Eater

Gulf Coast Paranormal Trilogy Series
Ghosted
Haunted
Dead
Spooked
Paranormal

Haunting Passions
Her Haunted Heart

Scary Fall Stories
Horrible Little Things

Seven Sisters
Seven Sisters
Ghost on a Swing

Twelve to Midnight
Mary Twelves
Pieces of Twelves

Standalone
Christmas at Seven Sisters
Delivered Me From Evil

Watch for more at www.mlbullock.com.

About the Author

Author M.L. Bullock enjoys the laid-back atmosphere and the spooky vibe of the Gulf Coast, especially the region's historic districts and sites. When she isn't visiting her favorite haunts in New Orleans or Old Mobile, you can find her flipping through old photographs or newspaper clippings in search of new inspiration.

Read more at www.mlbullock.com.